THE PIRATE PRINCE

LORDS OF THE VAR: A QURILIXEN WORLD NOVEL

MICHELLE M. PILLOW

MICHELLE M. PILLOW® - MICHELLEPILLOW.COM

Cat-shifter Prince Jarek sails the high sky doing what he pleases…that is until drug dealers kidnap one of his men. But the rescue mission goes wrong and instead of a crewman, he liberates a woman who he believes is desperately trying to escape her captors. He soon discovers he unwittingly kidnaped a princess.

Princess Mei has just learned her future from a seer, and it seems fate is giving her in marriage to a neighboring ruler. She will do her duty, but first she wants to experience an adventure. When the pirates come to steal, she knows exactly who she wants that adventure to be.

The Playful Prince
The Bound Prince
The Rogue Prince
The Pirate Prince

Captured by a Dragon-Shifter Series
Determined Prince
Rebellious Prince
Stranded with the Cajun
Hunted by the Dragon
Mischievous Prince
Headstrong Prince

Space Lords Series
His Frost Maiden
His Fire Maiden
His Metal Maiden
His Earth Maiden
His Woodland Maiden

Dynasty Lords Series

Seduction of the Phoenix
Temptation of the Butterfly

To learn more about the Qurilixen World series of
books and to stay up to date on the latest book list
visit www.MichellePillow.com

To the men and women, who risk their lives to make the world just a little bit better, be it military, law enforcement, firemen, or just your ordinary everyday heroes and heroines. And to the people who help others, no matter how small the task. To all of you, thanks.

Dragon Lords fans know the cat-shifting Var as being the villains of the story, but every conflict has two sides. With King Attor dead, it is up to the Var princes to pick up the pieces. Though these stories can be read as a standalone series, they do begin where the *Dragon Lords* left off, most significantly after *Dragon Lords 4: Warrior Prince.* There is also a prequel story, *Dragon Lords 9: The Dragon's Queen* that tells the story of how Attor became the cat-shifter king and how the Var-Draig war really started.

Lords of the Var® are interconnected to many Qurilixen World series installments, including: *Dragon Lords, Captured by a Dragon-Shifter* (the dragon-shifters and cat-shifters in modern day times), *Space Lords, Zhang Dynasty* and more.

To find out more about the books, including

reading orders, visit my website, www.MichellePillow.com.

As an added bonus in the *Lords of the Var*® series, see cameo appearances from some of your favorite *Dragon Lords* prince and princesses.

To stay informed about when a new book in the series installments is released, join my newsletter mailing list at: michellepillow.com/newslettersignup

KING ATTOR OF THE VAR

"A woman has the potential to be the ruination of men and
kingdoms.
The only question is, my son, will you let one ruin you?"
- King Attor of the Var

IMPERIAL PALACE OF THE ZHANG
DYNASTY, HONORABLE CITY,
MUNTONG TERRITORY, PLANET OF
LINTIAN

"YOU ARE WITH CHILD." The words were soft, carried as if on a gentle breeze.

Princess Zhang Mei blinked in shock, pausing in mid-action. She was in the process of setting down a jug of wine on the Sacred Chamber's altar as an offering to her deceased ancestor. Out of all the things her dead great-grandmother could've told her, that was the least expected. Her great-grandmother made a small noise when Mei didn't move to finish her task. Slowly Mei set the offering on the low round table and stepped back. For a long moment, she stared at the jug inlaid with gold thread in the blue glass. It was a pretty piece, one her great-grandmother would enjoy in her afterlife, but not as much as the wine it contained.

Mei wasn't frightened to see her great-grandmother's spirit. The ancestors were known to show themselves to those they wished to guide and, since her death, Zhang An had been residing in the sacred room hidden within the walls of the Hall of Infinite Wisdom located in their home, the Imperial Palace. Vast surrounding walls protected the palace. The compound behind the walls was referred to as Honorable City because the palace was in fact like a small city for the royal family. The family never needed to leave the palace and rarely did so.

The palace walls were surrounded on the outside by a thick moat with only two known entrances, one in the front and one in the back of the large rectangular complex. The Hall of Infinite Wisdom was only one of many buildings within the complex, located in the center. However, it was the largest structure, set high upon stone and towering over the surrounding courtyard and gardens.

Mei wished they left the city more often. Some of her best memories were from when she traveled with her sister, Fen. They'd often go to Lady Hsin's to see how the silk worms produced the luxurious silk for their clothing, or to the countryside, just to fly over in the family's *tu di hang*, a land craft that soared over the lush scenery like the ancient junk boats that used to sail over the seas of planet Old Earth.

But those times were too far apart to suit Mei. She'd been born with the need for adventure, a need that burned inside her until she was forced to swallow down her abhorrence of the palace walls. Burying her wanderlust, she knew that first and foremost, she was a Zhang princess and so would honor her family and do her duty by her people, no matter the personal cost. Besides, the confinement only made the trips she took all the sweeter, like the foray across the Satlyun River she was about to take with her oldest brother, Prince Haun.

Seeing her great-grandmother's face, Mei whispered, "What? What did you say?"

"You are with child," her great-grandmother repeated, smiling.

Mei stiffened. That's what she thought the woman had said. Why was the spirit smiling?

What did this mean? A baby? Her? Now? It didn't sound right. How could this…?

Dazed, Mei looked around the room. The Sacred Chamber was ornate, yet barren of all but a few objects of great importance. Gold lined the walls in an intricate design. The basin itself was carved with the revered phoenix of her people. Aside from the basin and offering table, there was the collection of the precious jade their ancestors had brought with them from Earth during the journey to Lintian. Its green color was sacred, more so than the purple jade mined across the river by Emperor Song's people. The artifacts were kept safe behind a plate of glass, the most precious being the powerful Jade Phoenix. The bronzed bird was surrounded by smaller pieces of the precious green stone. Its delicate feathers were fashioned in a way that should have been impossible in metal-work. Jewels were inlaid into the bronze, but none was as stunning as the large green stone on the bird's chest. To even look upon it was an honor, reserved for the royal family and a few honored souls.

"No, no I can't be," Mei insisted, feeling her flat stomach. "You are certain?"

"Yes. Very certain," Zhang An answered. The spirit was dressed in the old style. Her long sleeves swept over the floor as she walked near her grand-daughter. The delicate silk robe made even more so by the fact that it traveled on air. Every movement was silent, like the breeze. Her wrinkled, pale face was transparent, shading with each subtle move-ment, threatening to blow away completely. Long, dark hair streaked with white flowed around her shoulders. Tradition from her time of life would have been to wear it up, but An was proud of her locks and, being dead, wasn't dictated by such traditions. Besides, what could be done about it? She was already dead. "I consulted all the powers —the oracle bones, the divining basin, even the wind. Each say the same thing."

Pregnant? Me?

"But, how…?" Mei could barely move.

Her great-grandmother laughed. "You should speak to your mother as to the how. I only foresee the future."

Mei didn't find the woman very funny. She knew how, just not *how*.

How could this happen? And with whom?

"When?" Mei asked, shaking. She followed her floating great-grandmother with her eyes, afraid if she moved her locked knees she'd collapse in shock.

"Within sixteen moons, give or take," An answered, smiling.

Sixteen moons? That was only about eight months!

"Whose is it?" Mei pressed her hand tighter to her flat stomach and thought of all the men of the Muntong court. None of them appealed to her as a husband figure, but all of them would be willing to marry a Zhang princess. To deny her hand would be foolish indeed. She had the power of her family, money, land, and status.

"I see blood," her great-grandmother answered ominously as if going into a trance as the visions overtook her. Her dark brown eyes glazed over with white as she moved to a basin within the center of the sacred chamber. A cool breeze stirred the room as the woman asked the wind for answers. Her hair lifted all around her in a wild tangle of windswept fury.

Mei knew her great-grandmother listened to the elements because the wind also whispered to her. It was her gift, her power, bestowed upon her at birth by the Jade Phoenix. Mei could hear the promptings of the wind and, though her own talent wasn't as developed, she knew that it would whisper its secrets into her great-grandmother's ear. Often, she thought that was why she felt the need to be free, to fly like the wind because she had felt the presence in her since the cradle. As a child, she'd dream of flying, soaring high into the starry heavens. Mei wished the wind would take her now, right now, lifting her up and taking her past the palace walls to deep space where she could float for an eternity.

"Royal blood," An added in a monotone, drawing her mind back to Lintian. "The baby will be of royal blood."

"But I am royal, Grandmother," Mei said needlessly, trying to figure out the riddle that the future put before them. Sometimes Mei wished her family couldn't see the pieces. Often it created more confusion than it clarified.

Mei's stomach tightened, and she was afraid she'd be sick. Or was her great-grandmother implying Prince Song Lok? He was the son of the only other empire on Lintian, the Song Dynasty located across the Satlyun River. The river flowed through the center of their planet, separating the territories of Muntong and Singhai. Lok was the only male heir to the throne though he had three sisters—triplets. Mei had never met the Song daughters, and she'd met Prince Lok only once, a long time ago.

Not that there was any reason she would be introduced to the triplets. The two empires never really saw eye to eye. Emperor Song ruled the Singhai Empire in the west, and Mei's parents ruled the Muntong Empire in the east. In between the two territories was the Satlyun River, circling from north to south in the exact center of the planet of Lintian. The giant river was a marvel of nature, so wide it was impossible to swim across. It was one of the main reasons that the two empires did not fight. Though they didn't agree on much, peace was something the Lintianese cherished.

Was her marriage to Prince Lok going to ensure continued peace? Was that the real reason she was compelled to accompany her oldest brother, Haun, on his trip across the Satlyun? Was marriage talk in the works? What exactly was her great-grandmother not saying? Or was she saying it and Mei just didn't want to hear the words?

"The blood I speak of is not of the Zhang line. It is foreign." An gave her a pointed look.

Mei grimaced. Lok. She had to mean Lok.

"Married?" another voice intruded.

Instantly Mei stiffened as she turned at the sound of her father, the emperor's, voice. He wore a yellow robe decorated with red dragons and symbols. The red and yellow were the colors of royalty. It matched the buildings—all of which had yellow tiled roofs and dark red walls.

The emperor stood in the doorway, a look of supreme happiness on his face. If this were true, Mei would be the first of his children to marry. Her older sister, Fen, and four brothers, Haun, Jin, Lian and Shen had yet to take that step. Mei was the youngest and by all rights she should be the last expected to marry. That was how it was traditionally done.

This isn't fair.

"Yes," her great-grandmother answered. "And with child."

"You're sure?" the emperor asked, his smile widening as he looked down at his daughter's waist. The news pleased him greatly.

Mei touched her stomach, gasping, "No! We're

not sure. Honored grandmother was just going to look again."

"Yes," her great-grandmother put forth. "We are sure."

"No," Mei repeated. "We. Are. Not."

"This is a most happy day." Emperor Zhang beamed. The two elders ignored her as they spoke to each other.

"A most happy day," An agreed. "My grand-daughter should be told at once. She will want to hear this blessed news."

"Yes, the empress will be most excited to hear of Mei's wedding," the emperor agreed. "And most pleased by news of a grandchild."

At his words, a secretive look passed over her great-grandmother's face. Mei ignored it, unable to process anything else at the moment.

I'm going to have a child and get married? What?

She wasn't sure which was worse news, marriage or a baby. The truth was, Mei hadn't really considered either prospect seriously. Ever. To be married would be to remain tied to Lintian, even more so than she was now.

"No, it's wrong," Mei protested. She clutched her hand against her stomach. Her entire body shook, and she couldn't get past the fact that she was to have a baby. She wasn't ready for that. The husband she could deal with, if she had to, but the baby? Everything was happening too fast. "Do it again, grandmother. Please. Look again. I beg you."

An sighed, but moved to the basin to oblige. Running her hand over the cool water, she rippled it with her ghostly finger. A soft glow covered the woman's transparent features as her ethereal brown eyes again turned a milky white. "Positive. I see you large with child. A baby is to be conceived of royal blood. The next prince who is not of the Zhang bloodline whose path you cross will be both father and husband."

"Lok," the emperor whispered, confirming her fears. Her father's expression fell somewhat at the news of Prince Lok, but when he caught her staring at him, dumbfounded, he hid the look and again smiled. "Prince Lok is a fine choice. You are to travel to the Mountain Palace with your brother to meet with the Song family. It will be the perfect time for you to get to know him. I will not mention the prophecy to Emperor Song. Fate will take care of the details."

"But," Mei swallowed nervously, "I don't have to go. Am I really needed there? I just asked to go because—"

"You were compelled," her father said softly.

Mei bit her lip and dutifully nodded, even as

she thought, *because I wanted to get out of this place for a while.*

"You cannot run from fate," An said. "In the end, she will find you."

"But—" Mei tried to protest. "Fate has been changed in the past. Father, you said so yourself. Fate has been altered by those brave enough to fight her. Let me stay here this time."

"Those are merely stories, *mèimei*," her father said. "Folktales. They are used to teach lessons, not to be taken literally. Besides, we already told the Songs that you would be joining your brother. To back out now would be an insult."

"But, Father, aren't all tales based in truth? You once told me that—"

"I see no more and am drained," her great-grandmother interrupted. Mei opened her mouth to continue, but the breeze suddenly gusted around her and swept the old woman's figure over the offering of wine before both she and the drink vanished, pitcher and all.

"Many congratulations, my daughter," the emperor said, lightly patting her shoulder when they were alone. "This is a very fine match."

Mei's mouth opened, hanging slack as she tried to find the right words of protest. When her great-grandmother had summonsed her to the Sacred

Chamber, this was the last news she expected to hear. In fact, she'd hoped for quite the opposite—adventure and intrigue while visiting the Mountain Palace of Singhai. Instead, she got marriage and children.

"We don't know for sure," Mei whispered. "Great-grandmother could've read the future wrong. It's hard to interpret."

"Fate is just that, my daughter. Fate." The emperor gave her a smile of understanding. "And An has a great blessing. She would not speak if there were a chance she was wrong. You are to marry Prince Lok. Remember, these things do not happen without reason. Your marriage must be of great importance to our people and to theirs. It will seal the bond between us, a bond that could use sealing. Trust the fates to bless you with years of happiness and a joyous future."

Mei again opened her mouth. Swaying on her feet, a sensation of numb weakness came over her. She felt her father's arms around her as her body crumbled into a mindless heap, sucked into the blackness of denial.

2

SHAN GUNG DIN (Mountain Palace) of the Song Dynasty, Singhai Territory

Two weeks later…

Princess Zhang Mei kept her expression completely blank as she looked across the long table. It wasn't difficult. She'd been sitting on the floor for what felt like hours when, in fact, it had only been about thirty minutes. Cupping the small bowl of tea before her, she lifted it to her lips and sipped the hot liquid. It was spiced differently than she was used to, but was good nonetheless. After being in Shan Gung Din, she found many things were like that, different, but tolerable. It wasn't surprising, as both ways of life were derived from similar Old Earth cultures long ago.

How long until different becomes intolerable? How long

until the loneliness of being in a place where everyone thinks they're culturally superior to me sets in? How long until I'm forced to marry Prince Song Lok?

Mei glanced down at her stomach, knowing it wouldn't be very long at all if her great-grandmother's prediction were true. The sad thing was, An wasn't known for being wrong. When she dreamed of getting away from the palace, this wasn't what she'd had in mind. Suddenly, the idea of living anywhere else scared her.

The table they sat at was low to the ground, perfect for kneeling to dine. Low cushions padded her knees as she rested back on her legs. She was losing feeling in them, but they were at Emperor Song's palace of Shan Gung Din as guests, and she didn't dare insult him by wiggling in her seat.

Mei refused to dwell of her great-grandmother's prediction. Fate may be fate, but surely seeing the future was not an exact art. It was possible her great-grandmother misread. Not very likely, but possible.

Wasn't it?

Blessed ancestors, please be wrong.

Mei swallowed nervously, realizing she was dwelling when she'd just told herself she wasn't going to do that. She glanced again to Lok, who was across the table next to his father, Emperor Song. Every part of her wanted to put him off, to demand he stay away from her. Could she really be expected to have this man's child? To live in this palace with his snob of a father?

There was no doubt in her mind that the emperor was a snob. No, not just a snob. He was an elitist snob, and his son was little better from what she could tell. Though her father would be disappointed that she didn't want to marry Prince Lok, she knew he'd never force her. Forced and arranged marriages were a thing of the past though all marriages had to be approved by the royal astrologers before a proper union could be made. Normally, it was just for ceremony, though what was discovered could give great insight into the couple's future.

If not for her family's desire to make a favorable impression on the neighboring family, she'd have walked out long ago. Duty had been bred into her very soul, and she knew, that if fate truly had picked Prince Lok, then duty would demand she honor fate. However, if Lok didn't honor fate, that wasn't her fault. Was it? She didn't have to make him want her. There was no reason she'd have to go out of her way to please him.

Prince Lok was her social equal, raised much like she was. He was skilled in the ancient martial arts. With their background, she'd have expected they would have much in common, or at least something to discuss. However, when she was left alone with the prince, all he did was stare at her, his expression blank and his eyes probing. It was likely he didn't think the youngest daughter of Emperor Zhang was good enough for him.

I wonder if he'd consider any woman good enough for him. Mei made a face into her tea cup so they couldn't see.

Lok was the only male heir to the throne which would make him naturally picky. She would expect the same from Haun, though future emperor or not, Mei would never think anyone was good enough for her brother. She had yet to be introduced to Lok's triplet sisters. Since her stay was about over, she doubted she would be introduced to them at all. That in itself was a little rude of the Song family.

Mei turned her attention back to the Song men before her. Behind the two royals, a long row of *pu ren* waited to tend the table. The *pu ren* were hand-maidens who came to the palace to wait on the royal family and hopefully attract a husband of consequence from the guards. They were usually from noble or well-to-do households.

The Zhang family had their fair share of *pu ren* over the centuries, though none were employed at the Muntong court at present. Each of the women wore a *pien-fu,* an ancient style two-piece silk garment that was often used in old ceremonies when their people had lived on Earth. They varied in color but consisted of a tunic gown with long, square sleeves that extended to the knees and a skirt that reached to the floor. Even though some of the ancient Earth ways no longer applied to their modern culture, all of the Lintianese people clung to the traditions of the past.

Mei sat next to her brother, Prince Haun, the oldest child and heir to the Zhang throne. Haun was ten years older than her, but they'd always been close. Mei would be lying if she didn't admit that she had always idolized him. When she was a little girl, he'd been so strong and powerful. Now, as she was older, he was still those things, but she saw that he was also generous and kind. He would make a great ruler someday.

"Princess Mei," the foreign emperor acknowledged, his eyes roaming over her clothing.

Mei couldn't tell if it was approval or displeasure on his blank, bored expression though he did seem to look her over quite a bit. The Zhang were more modernized in style instead of the traditional fashions the people of Singhai preferred. Even so, her robe was belted tightly around her waist until it cut off her circulation. The *pu ren* had been sent to help her dress, and they'd insisted on cinching it tight. Not wanting to refuse Emperor Song's hospitality, she let them.

"You do not speak tonight," Emperor Song continued.

"Why speak when I would hear one of your lovely *pu ren* sing?" Mei answered, her voice low and sweet.

She saw her brother stiffen next to her and knew he was holding back his laughter. The little show she put on for the Song family was just that, a show. She was not meek or mild in her opinions or her convictions. However, she knew when to strike like a snake and when to be the timid, pretty flower. Mastering the art of both was what made her such a good negotiator. As the youngest and smallest of six children, negotiating had come in handy growing up. Otherwise, she'd have been teased mercilessly by her five siblings.

"Perhaps another time, sister," Haun said before the emperor could answer. "The boat waits for us."

Mei hid her sigh of relief. Haun knew of the prophecy and was saving her from enduring the Song family any longer. His negotiations were done for the most part, though whether he was satisfied remained to be seen. However, if it wasn't this negotiation, there would be something else with which he'd have to deal. Such was Haun's life and responsibility. Though nothing was said officially, the Zhang siblings had seen their oldest brother slowly taking over more and more responsibilities.

Haun stood, prompting the other men to do the same. Mei was the last to her feet. The stinging sensation of blood returning to her legs made her stand completely still though it took everything in her not to make a run for the docks. She'd made it through the ordeal without a proposal. The knot in her stomach began to lessen. This was it. Prince Lok had shown no interest. Her great-grandmother was wrong. She wouldn't have to marry him.

"You have honored us with your visit, Prince Haun," Lok said when his father didn't speak. Mei folded her hands in front of her, itching to get into a pair of silk pants and stretch her legs. The robe's thick belt only seemed to pull tighter against her ribs. "We will speak with the mining corporation about your family's concerns—"

"I assure you, there is nothing to be concerned about," the emperor interrupted, giving his son a stern glance.

"I'm sorry to disagree with you, emperor, but there is much to be concerned about," said Haun. "The Zhang people—"

"The Lin Yao mines have supplied our people with the sacred purple jade for centuries. The trade is too valuable and profitable to our dynasty. Why would we need to resort to manufacturing chandoo?" The emperor frowned, holding out his arms. "Do you presume to insult me? Do I look like a common intergalactic drug trader?"

"Not you, Emperor Song," Haun answered, not backing down. Mei was proud of him. The emperor was an intimidating man. "But maybe those within the Lin Yao Mining Company. When we analyzed the clothing taken from those on the ship, they were covered with traces of the mine dust. All we ask is that you look into it. Consider it a favor to the Zhang family."

The emperor's frown deepened as he looked down his nose at Haun. "I owe no favors to the—"

Lok placed a hand on his father's shoulder, but looked at the Zhang prince. "Please, we have been through this. We have heard your plea and will act. There is nothing further to discuss. I give you my word I will personally go to the mines and investigate these claims."

Mei studied Lok's hand on Emperor Song's arm. True, she didn't know the emperor or his family that well, but it seemed an odd gesture for the son to do. The emperor didn't say anything at the interruption but merely nodded once. The idea that Lok was taking over for his emperor, as Haun was for their father, struck her. In her head, she'd thought of marrying the Song prince, not the Song emperor. Lok's father wasn't an eligible husband, so his hand was never considered in the prophecy, but Lok would someday be emperor.

Empress Song Mei.

Mei trembled, as she thought of all her mother's duties. She did not want to be her mother. Yes, she loved the empress, but Mei had no desire to be the woman or to carry her royal burdens.

Haun bowed at the waist, his hands joined palm to fist in front of his chest. Mei dutifully nodded her head, though she wasn't addressed. The blood rushing through her ears drowned out sound as the men took their leave of each other.

Her brother stepped back from the low table and gestured for her to follow him. Mei did so without question, trailing properly behind him in respect. When they were alone, she hurried to his side. Taking a deep breath, she said suspiciously, "They hide something."

Haun quirked a brow but didn't answer.

"Prince Lok," she continued thoughtfully. "There was something odd about the way he was acting. I know we aren't acquainted with the man, but there was something..."

Haun still didn't respond.

"I know you think I'm crazy, but I sense that some——"

"The air has ears, and the walls have eyes,

mèimei." Haun's mouth drew into a faint smile even though his eyes stayed forward. "And right now my head is telling me you have no wish to marry the prince."

Mei sighed, saying no more as she nodded in agreement. He was right. Her judgment of the situation would be off due to her desire not to be there, not to have such a fate. She slowed her step, falling behind her brother as she followed him toward the palace docks. He was right. It was possible she was just fighting destiny and trying to find fault where there was none.

"*Zài-jiàn*, Shan Gung Din," she said under her breath, happy to be leaving the Mountain Palace. "Goodbye, Singhai Empire."

Haun glanced over his shoulder with a smirk, and she realized he'd heard her talking to herself. Without a word, he turned forward.

Mei smiled at his back as she continued on in silence.

3

"WHAT IN THE blazing star trails are we doing here, cap?" Evan Cormier grumbled, running his fingers through his short black hair. His eyes were focused on the great Lintianese palace before them. "What has that space cadet gotten us into now? I told him to leave that woman alone. I told him she was trouble, but can Rick ever see past his own lust? No! She batted her eyelashes at him and off he went like a little remloch mindlessly following a Grishelm floral dragon."

Jarek glanced at Evan and hid his smile. Evan was a good man to have on a crew, a hard worker and a hell of a smart guy. The man was part telepath, a fact he didn't share with too many, and it was those skills that Evan was referring to now.

Rick was the pilot on their ship, *The Conqueror*, and every inch a playboy. Evan had warned him against going with the dark-haired enchantress who had flirted with him on Leinad's star port where they'd stopped for fuel, but Rick hadn't listened. The enchantress had kidnaped him, for some reason still unknown to them, and taken him with her to the far reaches of the planet of Lintian. Though, knowing Rick, he'd opened his big mouth and said something stupid to insult her. It wasn't likely she'd taken him with her because she couldn't live without him.

So, now they were on Lintian to save him. Jarek knew Evan was irritated by this detour. They were all irritated by the detour, but Rick was their friend, and they would never leave him behind—no matter how stupid he'd acted which resulted in getting kidnaped by an intergalactic drug trader.

"We're here because we're rescuing Dev's best friend," Lochlann teased, dryly. He was the only crew member aboard *The Conqueror* from Jarek's home planet of Qurilixen. Jarek was a Var, a cat-shifter. Lochlann was a Draig, a dragon-shifter. Usually, the Var and Draig were at war, but Jarek had never seen a reason for it. It was why he'd left his homeland and why his good friend, Lochlann, had come with him. In the wide open skies of space, things like race didn't matter. Everyone was different.

Dev snorted at Lochlann's comment but said nothing. The group of men tried to contain their laughter. Dev was half Belvon, a demonic looking race with red skin and a very stern temperament. Aside from the intense coloring, he appeared humanoid, only larger. He was the ship's muscle and a bit of a loner. Rick was the polar opposite of Dev. The Belvon was all about maintaining order. Rick was all about breaking it. It often led to humorous fights. Sometimes when the crew was bored, they'd provoke them into an argument for the sake of entertainment. But, when it came down to it, if Rick was in trouble, Dev was there just like everyone else to bail him out. They were like a family.

A family of misfits, Jarek thought with a small chuckle. He wouldn't trade his life of freedom for anything in the world.

"I say we let Rick rot," Lucien mumbled, pouting. "Would serve him right for breaking my virtual girlfriend. Does he even realize how long it took me to get her breasts just right? And then he goes and melts all three of them off. Poor Fanessa!"

"Did you drink more Torganian Rum?" Viktor, Lucien's brother, demanded. The two constantly bickered but were actually quite close. If one said the sky was white, the other would swear it was black just for the sake of disagreeing. They were half human, half Dere, and had a milky white complexion that contrasted with the strangest red-brown and red-green of their eyes. Lucien was a communications genius, and Viktor was one hell of a mechanic. The man could rig anything. "We can't let him rot." Viktor paused. "He owes me space credits from that last card game."

"Yes," Jackson, a dark blond security officer, agreed. "And you owe me."

"Oh, right, yeah." Viktor cleared his throat. "I forgot about that. Well, how 'bout we cut out the middle man and just say Rick owes you?"

"Not likely," Jackson said. "He's not good for it and I'd rather not take your loss."

"Can we please concentrate on saving Rick? Then we can argue about who gets to kick his ass first," Jarek said, wondering briefly how he'd ever come to captain such a crew. Fate was funny that way.

They hid behind a long stone gate, looking up at the palace which was on top of a miniature mountain with a flat top. Long rows of stairs led up from the base, carved from the tan stone of the planet's earth. Their position was halfway up so they could easily see the front entrance. Platforms were carved intermittently along the stairs on the way to the top, decorated with black pots and golden statues inlaid with precious jewels. Jarek tensed. The Song Dynasty was a wealthy one. They must indeed have no fear of intruders if they put their treasure within plain view of the city below.

"One of us has to go in," Lucien said, eyeing Dev.

"Yes, I would make the obvious choice," Dev drawled, his tone heavy with sarcasm. With his giant red body, he was the farthest thing from the slender humanoid culture of Lintian.

Jarek tried not to laugh. Dev had been around Rick for too long and was beginning to pick up some sarcasm. Usually, the man was completely sober in nature.

"He's right, guys," Jarek said, "one of us needs to get in there and find out where the secret purple jade mines are located. My sources say that's where they've taken Rick."

All eyes turned back to the palace. The location of the mines wasn't known, no matter how much money he'd thrown down for the information. Most things about this planet were a mystery. Jarek could respect their desire for privacy. His home planet of Qurilixen was the same way. However, at the moment, it wasn't serving his purpose in finding Rick.

"Are you sure your sources are right? I hear tell that not even the greatest thieves can slip into this place," Lochlann said.

"Yeah, they guard their purple jade-like the Tog women protect their men," Viktor added. "Rick would have to get his ass dragged here."

Jarek frowned. He'd heard much of the same thing. Lintian was an isolated planet that many stayed clear of. The fact that its position was a long way off, combined with the rumored impossibility of breaching the security made it a daunting place, little worth a space traveler's time. Even if purple jade was valued quite highly, a pirate couldn't spend a fortune if he was dead. But they weren't here for jade. They were here for their friend.

"Why couldn't he have gotten kidnaped by Lord Maximus and taken to the Galaxy Playmates' mansion?" Lucien asked. "That way we could fight off half-naked playmates instead of these lethal warriors."

"Rick wouldn't want to be rescued from that," Lochlann said.

"Who would?" Jackson added under his breath. All of their eyes were still trained on the palace.

"I slipped through the city just fine earlier," Jarek said, hoping his men would take that to mean it was possible to get through. "Stealth is the key. This isn't the kind of place that you go in blasting. We'd never stand a chance against all those guards in a head-to-head fight. We're too outnumbered. Ideally, it's best if they don't know we're here."

The men nodded.

"Besides," Jarek continued, "no one has tried to breach these walls for centuries. Their guards have probably become lax. They won't be expecting us, especially not looking for a plain map. It should be a simple slip in and slip out type of job."

One long building made up the palace. It had tiled roofs with wide eaves that tilted up at the ends toward the sky. A long open walkway supported by columns was across the front of the large structure. An entranceway opened up in the center, leading inside the building or down a long row of steps to the outside world. Guards stood along the columned walkway, their loose fitting clothing very reminiscent of the Draig casual wear. It looked comfortable, yet military at the same time. The building seemed to grow out at the side into an enclosed hall, slowly working its way from the very top of the mountain down the side until joining to a lower building that had its own columned entrance and guards.

"It doesn't look like walking up to the front door and slipping in is going to be an option," Jarek said, eyeing the dark skinned warriors. Their long hair was pulled back in a single braid, keeping it out of their faces. They were slight in stature compared to the Var warriors, but he wasn't fooled. He'd seen some of them practicing in a field as they had sneaked into the city. They moved with such graceful ease and deadly precision when they fought, that Jarek knew they would be formidable opponents.

"I'll do it," Jackson said. "I'm the best climber, and if the inside of the palace is constructed like the outside, I should be able to make my way across the ceiling without notice."

"No, it's too risky. All someone would have to do is look up," Jarek denied the offer. "There are too many guards. Besides, we have no way of knowing what the inside looks like. The ceilings could be smooth with nothing to grab on to."

"That doesn't leave us too many options. If we can't infiltrate, we'll have to fight," Dev said softly. He opened his mouth to continue, but Lucien's voice interrupted him.

"Oh, my..." Lucien let loose a soft whistle. "Would you look at that tempting piece of Lintianese culture?"

Jarek immediately saw what had caught Lucien's attention. A slight female shuffled out of the palace, meekly following a taller man whose hair was knotted on the top of his head. The topknot seemed to be a popular style amongst the people. Jarek could instantly tell the man was royalty, or at least a nobleman, by the way he carried himself and by the way the guards bowed in respect. However, the guards ignored the woman.

Jarek couldn't look away from her. His heart sped in his chest and his breathing deepened. She was lovely. Silken robes hugged close to her small frame. Her long, dark hair was plaited and pulled up on both sides of her head.

"That's what I'm talking about," Viktor added, his voice soft.

"Yeah, no wonder you two like her," Lochlann teased, eyeing Viktor and Lucien. "She even makes you look muscular."

"We don't have time for concubines right now," Jarek said. Even as the words left his mouth, he found himself still staring at her. His gut tightened with desire. How could it not? She was gorgeous. Her downcast gaze lifted slightly and Jarek let his eyes shift with the power of the cat as he narrowed in on her. Like her people, her eyes were brown, a soulful color that begged for a man's protection, and shaped in such an exotically alluring way that he couldn't take his eyes off her. She was so deli-cate, like a flower. The woman even looked like a flower, dressed in flimsy silk. Small, circular patterns were spread over the robe she wore, intertwined with floral designs. It was a simple motif, yet captivatingly beautiful. Truth be told, Jarek found the whole planet beautiful. The landscape outside the palace was lush and green, and inside the city was clean and designed to enhance the beauty around it. Beneath the palace, the streets of the city were clean, and the people were immaculately dressed.

A tightness developed between his thighs, as Jarek became aroused just looking at the slender woman. Too bad she was obviously this other man's whore.

Maybe you could liberate her, his libido seemed to tell him.

And do what? His inner reason argued. *It's not as if you want a woman on the ship with you. You're not like your brothers. You're not meant to settle down.*

It was true. Jarek had felt it since he was a young prince. Even then he would stare up at the stars, feeling their pull. He wasn't meant to be contained on one planet. He needed more than that. He needed adventure, change, a sense of danger. Women liked things such as stability and a home. Sure, he'd met a few who didn't, but they were no one with whom he'd like to spend his long years. And, usually, in the end, even those women settled in one place.

Jarek had four brothers, and they'd all found mates. Three had just had babies, and his twin brother's wife was expecting. It wasn't as if he *needed* to find a wife and have children. The family line didn't depend upon him. He was free to do as he willed.

"She's so tiny," Dev said, his voice not holding as much masculine appreciation as the others. "And delicate. She wouldn't last five seconds in the VR fighting a Huthin."

"I don't want her as a sparring partner in virtual reality, space cadet," said Viktor. Dev's black eyes narrowed in warning. Viktor quickly patted Dev's large shoulder in reassurance. "And by space cadet, I mean my very big, mean, tough warrior friend who would never think of crushing someone smaller than himself, like me."

Dev grunted. Jarek bit back a laugh but didn't look away from the beautiful woman for more than an instant. She was close. The Lintianese man's body blocked her partially from view and he leaned to the side to better see her. Soft laughter broke into his daydreaming about the woman. A hand on his arm pulled him back down.

"Uh, Jarek, you still with us, captain?" Lucien

asked. "Or is your plan to get seen and captured? 'Cause if it is, please count us out."

Jarek motioned the men back, and they instantly crawled along the stone to stay hidden as the woman and her escort passed nearby, going down the overly long row of steps. Jarek watched from within an inlet in the wall as she moved away from them.

"I have an idea." Jarek grinned, still staring at the woman's backside. "I know just how one of you is going to get into that palace."

"How?" Viktor asked, leaning over to take his own peek at her.

Jarek's grin widened as he looked at Viktor and his brother. "Or should I say, the two of you."

"I can't believe you let Jarek talk us into this," Viktor hissed, pulling on his silk sleeve.

"Me?" Lucien demanded.

"Yeah, you!"

"Hey, this wasn't my idea," Lucien huffed, touching his cheek. "How's my paint?"

"Cosmetics," Viktor corrected.

"You would know," Lucien snorted at his brother. Both of them looked ridiculous, dressed as Lintianese women.

Instantly Viktor made a dive for his brother. Lucien crashed into the palace wall. They'd made it past the guards easily. Both of the warrior men had ignored them as the brothers shuffled in, walking as they'd seen the women of the planet do. It was easier than either of them had thought.

"Blessed stars, stop it," Lucien growled. "Someone's coming. Start acting all…*womanish.*"

Viktor instantly pulled back and began smoothing his robes. Lucien did the same, lowering his head and keeping an eye on the man who approached.

The man spoke but his words were in Lintianese, and neither of them had bothered to upload the language into their brain. He gestured to the side and began walking as if expecting them to follow. Viktor frowned and shrugged. The man looked back and said something again, this time louder.

Lucien glanced at his brother. "I guess we follow?"

"Great," Viktor drawled sarcastically. "But if he tries to slip a hand up my robe I'm leaving Rick to rot."

The brothers shuffled their feet as they followed the man. He waited impatiently, arching a brow before shaking his head. His eyes trailed over their feminine attire and a small shiver worked its way over his entire length.

When he turned, Viktor grimaced. Whispering, he said, "I don't know whether to be relieved or insulted by his repulsion."

Lucien rolled his eyes and gave his brother a shove to get going. Without saying another word, they trailed behind the man, down the ornate, golden palace hall.

4

MEI FOLLOWED HER BROTHER, lost in thought. The docks along the Satlyun were crowded with merchant ships. Close to the water was the space dock with small luxury crafts taking off and landing from the entrance to the long stone building. The ships could be seen drifting across the light blue skies, some of the older ones leaving cloud-like trails in their wakes. It was a beautiful sight.

Wide wooden ships lined the banks of the river. For her, seeing the two so close together was normal, but it was still an odd contrast between the old ways and the new. Even though the boats looked traditional, they were modern in every way, with the ability to hover over the water when the waves got too rough. Mei sometimes wished they couldn't so that they could ride the water and everything it gave them, rough or not. At least it would be an adventure.

"Not the true love you expected when great-grandmother told you of your future, *meimei*?" Haun arched a brow as he stopped close to where the Zhang royal ship was docked. "Prince Lok seemed to be a strong enough warrior to me, but what do I know of picking men for my sister to marry? To me, none of them are worthy of you."

Mei turned her attention from the bobbing mast to study her brother. She just wanted to leave the Singhai Empire behind her. Forever. "You are not funny, *gē ge*."

At the moment, part of her wanted to leave her home planet forever. But, looking at her brother's dark eyes, she knew she'd miss never seeing him again. She was too close to her family.

"I feel your soul, *meimei*, and I know your heart." Haun chuckled, his lip twitching up at the side as he pulled her to him in a brief hug. She rested her head on his comforting chest before he let go, and she was compelled to step back. Haun opened his mouth to continue, but a loud shout from the Song palace interrupted him. Automatically he lifted his arm to block her from whatever the commotion was. Mei leaned over to see past him.

Two women ran from the palace with what

looked like well over a dozen of the Song guards giving chase. Their robes trailed behind them, disheveled and very indecent. Mei was sure she could see flashes of their flat chests and bare legs.

"What's happening?" Mei asked, frowning.

"I don't know." Haun took a step forward, his body tense as he readied for a fight.

Suddenly, five men appeared on one of the decorative platforms along the side of the stairs. The group of men joined the women in the race down the mountain. They weren't dressed like the males of her planet and, in fact, they looked like space rogues. She'd seen plenty of pictures of pirates growing up. Emperor Zhang had insisted all his children be well educated. Mei stiffened, intrigued. The most noticeable was a giant red man dressed all in black. Next to him were several humanoids.

"They steal the emperor's *pu ren*," Haun said. He lifted his hand to the boat, motioning the Zhang guard down to his side. "Get in the boat, Mei."

"No, wait," she protested.

"Get her in the boat," Haun ordered the guards, grabbing her by the arm and thrusting her toward them. She stumbled, taken by surprise at his grip. He was only trying to protect her, but it was still annoying to be told what to do.

"Haun," Mei protested, screaming at him as a couple of Zhang guards caught her by the arms and pulled her toward the docking plank. "Get off me. I can protect myself."

The guards didn't listen. Mei knew it was pointless to struggle, but she did anyway. The tight bodice of the gown kept her body stiff and her protests ineffective. The guards kept going. They were trained to take the future emperor's order before hers. Anything Haun said would supersede any protest she made.

"Haun," Mei yelled.

Haun ignored her. He stepped forward with the Zhang guards as the thieves came down the docking plank chased by the Song men. Mei was thrust aboard the ship. She refused to go down below as she watched from the railing. A soft breeze blew around her, lifting her clothing behind her as it pressed the silk to her stomach and chest. Her guards, obviously wanting to see the capture, didn't protest her choice of location as they stood at her side in protection.

Mei grasped the railing, itching to be part of the fight. Being a princess, it wasn't often that she saw any action. One of the pirate thieves grabbed onto a handrail and wrapped his legs over it, sliding past the remaining steps. A few others followed suit, including one of the women whose silk gown ripped loudly as she landed none too gracefully. Without missing a step, the big red man grabbed the woman by the arm and hauled her to her feet as he passed by. The woman limped slightly next to him, but he thrust her forward, and she kept running.

Who were these women? They didn't move like normal *pu ren*. Had Emperor Song obtained them from a foreign planet? Were these their people coming to rescue them?

Mei shook her head, automatically dismissing the idea. Emperor Song was too much of a snob to take foreign women into his bed. However, she could see him kidnapping women from his own countryside…

No, Mei, don't you dare think it. That's not fair, and you're just bitter about the idea of marriage.

As the thieves came closer, she got a better look at them. A dark one with long black hair caught her eye. Black markings were on his neck, and she wondered briefly what they stood for. His locks were pulled neatly back into a single rope that flew behind him like a long body of a festival dragon. A woman by the man's foot tripped, and he grabbed her up, thrusting her toward the big red fellow. The large man caught the *pu ren* up easily without missing a step and followed the other thieves.

One of the Song guards leaped, flying through

the air to catch up to the band of criminals. The man with the neck markings turned to face him. The other thieves kept running. The long haired man shouted an order for them to get somewhere. Mei tensed, recognizing the language. It was a star language, not of Lintian. She'd uploaded it years ago, and it took her brain a moment to translate the words.

"Pirates," Mei whispered, her heartbeat quickening in excitement as she realized they really were pirates. She glanced up, looking around the ship for something to use to escape her guards and get down to the fight. If she didn't hurry, it would be over.

Another shout sounded. The man with long hair squared off against the Song guard. He was tall, much taller than the warriors he faced, though not as big as the red giant. The man's height was only all the more intimidating because of his massive girth. The foreign clothing he wore was revealing, the shirt tight to his chest as it moved like a second skin against him. Laces crossed over his sides, revealing the flesh of his waist. Snug breeches clung to his hips and legs. His arms were strong and muscled, showing that he worked out often. They joined onto broad shoulders and a thick chest. His physique intrigued her, and she watched eagerly to see how he would fight. Already by his stance, she determined he wasn't trained as her people in the ancient technique of martial arts.

There was something wild and arrogant about the way he faced the Song guard. He was fearless, bold. His fist balled as he stalked forward, punching the guard square in the jaw. The Song warrior flew back from the sheer force of the blow. A second guard charged as he caught up to the pirate, drawing back his foot to snap out at the thief with a jumping front kick. The pirate blocked it but was hit in the chest by another Song guard. He stumbled back, but didn't fall. The pirate had absorbed the blow, instantly finding his footing to knee the warrior in the stomach. The guard stumbled, and the pirate sprinted off before any more warriors caught up to them.

Haun stood apart from the Song warriors, out of the way as he watched and waited. Until the Zhang were invited into the fight, they would not get involved. But, by standing ready, they offered their services to their Song host as duty required of them.

Mei glanced around. Something outside of herself compelled her to move when she knew she should not. It was like a whisper in her ear, carried by the breeze, telling her to confront the thief. Instinct kicked in. It was a feeling of desperation. She needed this fight, needed to feel the blood pumping in her veins. If her destiny was truly a life at Shan Gung Din, then she would face it head on with courage. Maybe this was the deed that would bind her to Prince Lok. In that moment, nothing mattered. The breeze grew stronger, carrying the sting of the cold water with it. Her senses spun. The wind took over, urging her to act.

The two who guarded her barely gave her a second glance as she pulled back from the ship's wooden rail. Seeing a rope, Mei grabbed a knife from beneath the folds of her skirt. She sliced through it, wrapping the thick cord around her wrist as she ran for the boat's side. Jumping, she soared over the guard's head with her blade gripped tightly in her free hand. The bodice of her gown made graceful movements difficult, and she kicked in the air trying to stop her body from spinning. The guards yelled at her, but she was too fast for them.

Mei flew over her brother's head, swinging in an arch through the air, out of Haun's reach. She kicked her feet, trying to control her descent. Her body veered toward her target, the pirate thief, and she aimed her feet at him.

"Zhang Mei!" Haun yelled, his tone irritated with her and scared at the same time. She couldn't answer as she concentrated on her target.

Twisting in the air, she flung her legs around, so

her stomach faced the ground as she let go. She flew head first at the pirate. Time seemed to slow the instant his eyes met hers. The brown pupils were so dark his eyes could've been black. He looked surprised to see her and held his arms out as if he planned on catching her instead of fighting her. Mei gripped the knife, holding tight. She didn't want to hurt him but subdue him.

At the last second before impact, she tucked her body and slammed into the man's chest. He grunted as they fell, rolling beneath her so he could absorb the brunt of their tumble. The second they hit the ground, the pirate rolled on top of her, crushing her with his weight. His large palm shackled her wrist, holding her knife hand firmly against the ground. Mei barely glanced at it. Her arm was slack, and she didn't want to fight him. Every instinct in her screamed not to hurt him. He was bigger than she had anticipated from the distance, his body hard with muscle as it pushed into hers. Her senses took in everything—his firm lips, his dark eyes, his proud straight nose.

Mei's eyes again met his as he tried to pin her free arm. His hot breath fanned her cheek, and his lips were close. Gold flickered through his gaze as he looked at her, and she felt every hot inch of him in that second as he held her down. He succeeded in trapping her wrists, only to gracefully jerk back and haul her to her feet at the same time. Her knife stayed on the ground.

At the motion, her mental functions clicked back on, and the sudden cloud lifted. Mei was pissed that her blow hadn't leveled him more. How could this man absorb so many kicks and still remain standing? The Song Imperial guards were some of the best fighters on the planet of Lintian, and yet this pirate took all they gave and kept going like he was unstoppable.

Or on drugs.

"Hey, *fea*, I appreciate your enthusiasm, but now isn't the time for such things." The man's tone was low and dripped with sweetness. Mei frowned at his arrogance, but he merely continued, "I promise you that later, if you still want to continue this, I'll be happy to help you out of that very alluring gown and onto something more comfortable."

Mei gasped in shock at what his words implied, instantly glancing down to what he wanted to 'help' her onto. No man had ever dared to talk to her in such a way. She answered in the star language he used, but her words were thick with the accent of her people, "Now is...the perfect time...to halt you."

"Captain, come on. Time to fly!"

Mei looked over the arrogant pirate's shoulder only to find the red man waiting for them. She heard a footfall behind her and knew her brother was running to catch up to her. With the stunt she'd pulled, she'd landed far away from where he stood. Swinging her leg around, she tried to kick the man's legs out from under him. It would've worked, but the red man appeared at her side and grabbed her easily into his strong embrace, lifting her off the ground.

"If you wanted to come with us, all you had to do was ask," the dark haired man, who was obviously the captain of the pirates, said with a wink as she struggled to be free of the burly red man's hold. He leaned over, picking up her knife only to shove it into his waistband. "Dev, get her onboard the ship. We'll figure out what to do with this one later. It's getting too heated down here."

Mei blinked. Even though she took in every detail of the encounter, it only took a matter of seconds before she was being hauled off on the red man's shoulder. She opened her mouth, but the jarring movements against her stomach kept the words from coming. Dev was too strong, and she couldn't get free. Pushing up, she saw her brother running after them. Behind him was the mountain palace of Shan Gung Din. Suddenly, she didn't want to be free. She pretended to fight but didn't use all the moves she knew to get loose from the giant. Part of her wanted to be gone.

When she had jumped off the royal Zhang ship, she hadn't intended to get caught. But, now that she was, she was going to let them take her. She tried to reason that it was because she wanted to save the *pu ren* they stole. However, she knew she was lying. She wanted to run from the future her great-grandmother laid out for her. She wanted to run from Prince Song Lok.

5

Jarek didn't want another passenger, but what else could he do? Leave the little woman to be beaten for an attempted escape? The poor thing was so scared of her owner that she'd risked her life jumping off his ship.

Besides, he'd be lying if he said he wasn't attracted to her. There had been a moment when their eyes met, right as she was flying at him. The dark brown of hers connected with his, and he felt a shock all the way to his gut. It was blinding, liquid desire. For that second, his blood had slowed in his veins, so thick his heart couldn't pump it. He'd opened his arms to her, unable to do anything else. Then she'd hit him like a phazer blast to the chest, knocking the wind from his lungs and consequently knocking his senses back into his head. In the midst of escaping from Imperial warriors was definitely the wrong time to be mentally undressing flying women.

Even when they look as delectable as she does.

Jarek glanced over his shoulder to check on her, as he ran toward where they had *The Conqueror* cloaked from view on top of the space dock building. Dev carried the slender woman. Her master was close behind them, shouting angrily.

With Jackson's innate climbing ability, the man reached the top of the building first and tossed down a rope ladder for the rest of them. By the time the others reached the roof, the engines had kicked. Jackson leaned over the side, motioning Jarek and Dev to hurry.

Hearing a noise, Jarek turned as they reached the ladder.

"*Ni shi bai chi!*" the little woman over Dev's shoulder yelled as Jarek motioned for the man to go first. Jarek didn't understand her and didn't have time to analyze the tone. By the dialect she spoke, it was hard for him to decipher her mood by the tone of her voice anyway. "*Yang gui zi!*"

"Hold on, *fea*, we're getting you out of here," Jarek assured her, assuming she was scared. He turned to the side, seeing the guards running toward them. "No reason to be frightened. We do this all the time."

"That's not—*umph!*" Her yell was cut off by Dev's jarring movements as the man scaled the building by the rope ladder still carrying her.

Dev was on the roof in a matter of seconds, and Jarek climbed up right behind him. As he neared the top, the palace guards caught up to them.

"Hurry it up," Jackson yelled, reaching over the side to pull Jarek up by his arm. Then, taking the knife the woman had dropped in her escape, Jarek sliced the rope ladder. The guard half way up the side fell, taking the others with him as they tumbled to the ground.

Jarek laughed, saluting the fallen men. Then, his eye caught the noble who'd been leading the woman around, her master. His face was contorted with anger as he ran for the building. Jackson pulled Jarek's arm to get his attention. Everyone was already onboard the ship as he followed Jackson to the loading dock.

"Go, go, go," Jarek ordered, jumping on as the door was closing. He looked out onto the rooftop. Just before the narrow slit of the closing door blocked his view, he caught a glimpse of the woman's owner landing on the building, as if he had jumped from the ground.

"Super nebula," Jackson swore. "Did you see that?"

Breathing hard, Jarek laughed, resting on the metal floor of the cargo hold. Excitement pumped in his veins, invigorating him like nothing else could. The ship jolted as they took off. A box slid across the floor, bumping his leg but it didn't hurt. He knew Lochlann was most likely piloting the craft and trusted the man to get them out of there. Looking up from his prone position, he ordered Jackson, "Go and check the engine. Stay with it until we're clear. I don't want anything happening like in Alphet principality. We can't afford to have the engine blow out if they give chase."

"On it." The man was instantly on his feet, running to do as Jarek bid.

Taking one last deep breath, Jarek kicked the box away from him and climbed to his feet. The ship shook, knocking him around as he stumbled toward the cockpit. Bright lights lit the corridor, running in intermediate strips like arches along the walls and overhead. Jarek slammed against the metal wall, only to be thrown to the opposite side a second later. The ship angled, and his feet slid as if the gravity controls were slipping. Lochlann soon had the ship righted, and he was able to continue on.

"Gun dan!"

Jarek heard the rescued woman screaming and grinned.

"Daì ruò mù jī!"

Poor thing was probably scared out of her mind from all the action. Being captain, it would be his duty to comfort her later. But, for now, he had an Imperial army to outrun.

Reaching the cockpit, he nodded at Evan in the co-pilot seat. Lochlann was in the middle of switching controls as they broke the planet's atmosphere.

"Bravon's Furnace, Evan," Lochlann growled, even though he grinned. Each one of them loved the adrenaline rush brought on by such things as outrunning guards. "You couldn't see that one coming?"

"I can read people, not predict the future, space cadet," Evan said good-naturedly.

"We've got a ship coming fast." Lochlann pointed to a transparent navigation monitor that floated above the console. It showed their position and that of other ships. "Straight up our asses."

"It's Lintianese," Evan confirmed with a touch to the ship's computer panel. The craft's round design was distinct, giving it away instantly. "And the bad boy doesn't look happy to see us go."

"Always wanting to wine and dine us, aren't they?" Jarek laughed. He grabbed hold of the back of Evan's chair, as Lochlann took an evasive turn. Staring at the screen, he ordered, "Do whatever you have to, Loch, but get us out of here."

6

"*SHEN JING BING*," Mei yelled at the red demon who tossed her on the small bed. The ship jerked, signifying a rough atmospheric change. They'd reached space. She knew what it felt like because she'd left orbit before. It had been just another part of their education, piloting space crafts in case of emergencies.

The room was tiny, especially compared to what she was accustomed to. It was rectangular and constructed mostly of metal, lacking the luxury of decoration and design. However, the bed looked comfortable, and there was enough space to move around in. A small decontaminator was built adjoining the room. By the looks of it, the pirates weren't very rich. She could tell by the ship's style, and the fact that it had been on the roof of the docking building, that it wasn't a Lintianese vessel. Finishing her quick assessment, she turned to her captor, the red giant.

Dev grinned. He wore all black. The color matched his eyes and his short cropped hair. It actually looked stunning next to his red skin. "I assure you, my lady, I am quite sane."

Mei paled. He understood her? She'd been yelling obscenities at him since before they boarded the ship. She just assumed none of them knew what she was talking about. Blushing, she took a deep breath. Watching him carefully, she made sure he wasn't going to try anything. His stance wasn't leering or sexual so she doubted that would be his intent. Good thing for him. She knew about a dozen ways to rid a rapist of his manhood.

"And I highly doubt you have the anatomy you claim to possess, let alone truly wish for me to put it in my mouth." Dev's grin widened as if he could read her suspicions. He looked like he was teasing her, but Mei was frightened by him and could merely stare, concentrating on hiding her emotions. The red man straightened his back, his black eyes taking her in. "Forgive me, my lady. I am *Salebinaben Johobik en Dehauberkelsain en Thoraxian en Yyrtolzx Devekin.*"

Mei frowned in concentration. He spoke so fast.

Slowly, she repeated, *"Salebinaben Johobik en Dehauberkelsain en Thoraxian en....*

"...Yyrtolzx Devekin." Dev nodded, looking impressed. "But you may continue to call me *shen jing bing* if it makes you feel better."

"Your leader calls you Dev. I shall use that." Mei lifted her chin, giving him her most regal look. "Now, I will know by what right you kidnap me and Emperor Song's *pu ren.*"

"You'll have to ask the captain. I was just following orders." Dev nodded, backing out of the door. He lifted his hand to the door sensor.

Before he could shut it, she asked, "You know who I am? You said 'my lady'."

"All women aboard this ship are a lady. Captain's orders," Dev answered, running his opened hand across the sensor. The door slid shut between them.

Mei took a deep breath. Was the title mocking of their prisoners? She doubted it was said in respect.

Shivering, she thought of the pirate captain. As she was forced onto the ship, she had a good view of the man, perhaps more than she wanted as Dev held her upside down. By her guess, he was a human male, or in the very least a humanoid. His eyes had glowed with gold flecks signifying there was some other kind of blood in him. If she had her guess, she'd say he was a shifter of some sort. The thought thrilled her. She'd read of shifters, but had rarely seen an actual shift.

Mei hated to admit that the man intrigued her on a very primal level. She wasn't stupid. She knew what lust and desire were. She'd even had a few lovers in her lifetime, even though she was still young, only forty-seven years of age. It wasn't as if she had been conceived that very morning. Though, in her experience, men usually came with more strings attached than she liked.

Looking around the room, she shivered anew. The walls bore down on her as the impact of her decisions hit her full force. In the midst of the fight, all she could do was think of how she wanted to be in on the action. The wind had stirred, calling her, telling her to go. The element was a wicked temptress. It always had been to Mei. The wind got inside her and urged her to be free, just as it was, blowing wherever and however it willed.

Then, as she was lying beneath the strong pirate captain, she'd just wanted to be free of her duty, of the Song palace, of her future with the stoic Prince Lok. She wanted the freedom that the pirate captain represented. And, there was no denying it, she wanted the pirate as a lover. There was danger and excitement in him, a sense of the unknown. The intoxicating power of it overwhelmed her blood, making her heart beat so fast she could barely breathe. There was a seduction to that facet of his appearance. He was everything she shouldn't have, but he did represent, albeit to the extreme, everything she'd ever wanted.

But now, the reality of what she had done was setting in. There were some impulses that shouldn't be followed.

She was a princess. These were pirates. What would they do if they found out who she was? Would they ransom her? Sell her into slavery on the black market at the Torgan sex slave auctions? A princess would undoubtedly fetch a high price for such men. Then why had the wind whispered to her to go? Did this ship have something to do with her fate in marrying Prince Lok? Was this her way to deny fate? Would she have to trade her family, her life, and her home for freedom? Even as she thought it, she knew she couldn't do that. She would never give up her family and her homeland, even if that meant marrying a man she could never love. If fate needed her to marry Prince Lok, she would do her duty and marry him. There was more to life than marital bliss and love. She would comfort herself with that. And, hopefully, a mutual affection would grow between them in time.

The ship jerked erratically and she knew they were making a rough getaway from her brother's men. Haun would not sit idly by while the pirates took his sister. What if he was hurt rescuing her? What if they shot at him? What if he was killed? How could she ever live with herself?

"Blessed ancestors," Mei whispered, gripping the soft blanket that covered the bed as the ship shook wildly back and forth. "What have I done?"

7

Jarek slid into Evan's chair as the man ran to join Jackson in the engine room. They'd lost power when the Lintianese starship had pelted them with shocks of energy. The large viewing screen before them blurred as they sped through the stars. It took almost all of the ship's energy just to keep up the high speeds.

"Who in the star blazes is that woman?" Lochlann growled.

"Wealthy man's concubine," Jarek answered, reaching to divert energy from the life support system to the thrusters. The corridor lights dimmed.

"I envy you then," Lochlann laughed, not looking over from where he manned the ship's controls. There was a preoccupation to his tone as he maneuvered the ship.

"Why's that?" Jarek asked. A magenta haze grew across the viewing screen.

"Well, if she's worth this much firepower, she must be good in bed." Lochlann flashed a wide grin. Another shock of energy hit, shaking them. "Bloody nova, I wish Rick were here."

"If he were, we wouldn't be in this mess," Jarek said.

"Ah, perfect irony that," Lochlann agreed.

Another blast hit the ship, jarring them.

"Sacred cats! Just get us out of here." Jarek ran his hand over the computer sensors, bringing up the floating screen. Scrolling through star charts, he looked for a place to hide from the Lintianese.

"And where would you have me go?"

"There," Jarek said, pointing to the large viewing screen in front of them.

"I don't see anything."

"Just fly, Loch. Trust me."

Lochlann turned the ship and headed straight to where Jarek pointed.

"Hold on!" Jarek yelled over the ship's intercom as he typed coordinates into the computer. Lochlann let go of the controls. The ship realigned, and suddenly the streaks of light were swirling around them even though the ship felt like it was flying straight. Closing his eyes against the dizziness the sight brought on, Jarek held tight, knowing that the ship was no longer in their control.

"By all the gods," Lochlann swore. "We're in a magefeld!"

"Yeah and it's about to get rough so hold on," Jarek ordered.

Just as the words were out, the ship started to shake, jerking erratically back and forth. Something clanged behind them in the corridor, rolling along the metal floor only to come crashing back as the ship flipped over. The motion was so fast, it glued them to their seats with the force. Jarek had never been so glad for gravity control in his life. Otherwise, they'd all be on the ceiling.

As quickly as it began, the ride stopped with an abrupt jerk. They both flew forward, hitting the consul. The ship jarred as their hands hit some of the controls, but they easily righted it. Jarek took a deep breath as he reached for the controls. After a quick check, he said, "We've lost them."

"Checking systems now," Lochlann paused then swore. "We're in for some repairs."

"Maybe the woman will know something useful about Lintian." Jarek thought of the slender woman, trying to put his desires for the fairer sex aside as he concentrated on what had to be done. "She might know the mines."

"Where are we?" Lochlann asked, getting up to lean over the controls.

Flipping through the star charts, Jarek stopped as he found the right one. "Somewhere along the edge of the X quadrant. Surfing the magefelds isn't exactly a precise science. They just spit you out wherever they want."

"Wonderful. There are only about a million port locations to choose from," Lochlann drawled. "I'll get working on a location. We need fuel and then we need to get back to rescuing Rick."

Jarek's jaw tightened. Every minute they were away from their friend was a minute they didn't necessarily have to waste. Though none of them wanted to admit it, they knew there was a real possibility that Rick was already dead. They might joke about killing him, but the truth was they loved him like a brother. In an odd way, joking about it kept them from dwelling on their worries.

"He's alive," Lochlann assured Jarek, placing a hand on his arm. "If there is any man that could charm a kidnapper, it's Rick."

Jarek nodded. He'd taken to the skies to be free of responsibility. Back home, his family had matters well in hand and managed just fine without him. The irony was that, as captain, he had more responsibility than he would ever be given on his home world of Qurilixen.

Rick was part of that responsibility. And even though the man had got himself into the mess, Jarek knew he had to get him out of it.

"Now, about this prisoner you took," Lochlann hid a smile as he turned to the charts. He began flipping through them, searching.

"She's not a prisoner. She practically hung onto my neck to get away from her master."

Lochlann glanced back at him and raised a brow before turning to his work once more.

"It's true," Jarek insisted. "She all but begged me to take her. What else could I do? Leave her to be beaten for trying to escape? Honor would not allow it."

Lochlann laughed, shaking his head. Without bothering to look, he asked, "Honor? Or your libido?"

Jarek harrumphed. "You're impossible."

"Aye."

"I'm going to see what damage has been done to the engines," Jarek left the cockpit, knowing that Lochlann would alert him if there was any sign of danger.

"Damage to the engines or the new cargo?" Lochlann called behind him.

Jarek stopped, leaning to peek back into the

cockpit. "Did I say impossible? Make that a pain in my ass."

"Aye," Lochlann agreed with a mischievous grin.

8

"I DEMAND you release me and the others."

Jarek looked at the small woman before him. That was hardly the greeting of appreciation he expected walking into her room. Her accent was thick, but he found he rather liked the smooth silk of her tone. It was almost husky in her anger toward him.

"I said, I demand that you release me and the other women you have taken."

Jarek crossed his arms over his chest and studied the woman. She was beautiful, so much so that his body ached for something beyond her anger. Her eyes flashed, and her body was rigid. Leaning against the metal frame of the door, he tried to act nonchalant. In truth, he felt as if he couldn't breathe.

"Do you not understand your own language? I demand release and also for the others." Her lips moved, carefully forming each syllable.

Jarek's mouth jerked into a grin. She demanded release did she? By the look on her face, he knew the type of release he was thinking of wasn't what she had in mind.

"Where are the others?" The woman took a menacing step forward, bracing her feet.

"Others?" Jarek repeated, confused. Then, laughing, he thought of Viktor and Lucien dressed as women. She must have seen them making a run for it. "Ah, yes, the others. They are perfectly safe and happy to be onboard."

"I shall be the judge of that. I demand you take me to them!"

"You know, for a servant, you really are demanding," Jarek mused. "Is that what your master likes? To be ordered around?"

"Servant?" the woman gasped, before quickly amending. "Yes, servant. What of it?"

Jarek studied her. He'd been mistaken about her. She wasn't a servant. Those who served didn't look so proud, didn't stand so bold and defiant. Her gaze was too sharp, too quick to look him in the eye. Even a defiant servant would look down, glaring through the sides of their lashes. Not her. She met him straight on. He'd been mistaken in his assessment. She was most likely a noble as well. Sister? Wife? Or, what if she were a concubine, a head concubine? Whatever it was, she was used to being listened to by others.

"What is your name, servant?" he asked, taking a bold step in. If she wanted to play this game, he'd play. The woman didn't back down, furthering his belief that she was more than she pretended to be. Then why come aboard his ship if she had power?

"You first, pirate."

Pirate? Jarek tried not to laugh. He never considered himself a true pirate, though some of the things he and the crew did were borderline criminal. Since she was lying to him about who she was, why not return the favor? "Captain Jarek the Handsome, very much at your disposal, my lady."

"I'm not a lady," the woman said carefully. "I'm just a servant."

"Ah, well, you have two legs instead of three, so that makes you a lady on this ship." Jarek grinned. It took a moment, but he detected the instant his meaning sank in. Her face turned dark red, and she gasped, unable to answer. Her eyes darted down to his thighs. He shifted his weight, trying to hide the effect her intense stare had on his shaft. It was no use. The mass between his thighs filled and pressed indecently against his tight pants. There was no concealing his desire for her.

She's a noblewoman, he thought, knowingly, as he witnessed her look.

"Tell me, servant, in what ways did you serve your master? Had you a specialty?" he asked, purposefully letting his tone dip in sexual meaning. A shiver worked its way down her slender form as he looked her over. He watched her nipples bud against her silk robe and her toes curled beneath the softer material of her ground shoes. Electricity snapped between them, hot and potent. By the look in her eyes, she knew it as well. The chemistry had been instant, connecting them. He wanted to pounce, to act, but he held back, knowing pleasure would only be heightened by denial.

The woman took a moment before saying carefully. "Royal cook."

She expected him to believe that the Imperial guards chased them for a cook? Jarek chuckled. So be it.

"Wonderful. The food simulator is acting up. It gives raw ingredients, and we are in need of a cook on the ship until we can get it fixed. You may pay your way with such service, that is, unless you have something else in mind?"

"Pay my way?" she questioned.

"Yes, as our ship's cook. Unless there is some other service you'd like to offer up in exchange for passage?" Jarek stepped boldly forward, again caressing her with his eyes. His stomach tightened in instant protest of the sexual denial. His hands balled into fists on their own accord, as claws tried to grow from the tips of his fingers. He knew the beast was in his eyes, but he couldn't call it back. He smelled her reaction. There was a trace of fear, but mostly interest. This woman wasn't frightened by the hint of the cat inside of him. Just knowing she wasn't surprised by his shifting side excited him more.

"What do you mean I must pay my way? You kidnaped me, pirate." Her lips tightened in displeasure. "Since when does the victim have to pay for being taken? If anything, it is your responsibility to see to my care."

"Yes, and perhaps we should work on your understanding of my language. I have the uploads onboard if you need them. First, you must not have been kidnaped before, because nowhere in the pirate code does it claim we have to take care of you, and that you don't pay your way. In fact, it is quite often the opposite for those taken. Second, and most importantly, I didn't kidnap you, *fea*, I rescued you."

"My name is not *fe-ah*. It is—"

"What does it matter, cook?" he interrupted just to aggravate her. She was adorable when she was mad. He found himself wanting to smile but suppressed the urge.

True, the woman was entertaining, but he didn't want to get too attached. Already, he felt something in her presence he rarely felt with women…kinship, perhaps? There was an odd feeling of easiness, even as they fought. Maybe he'd been in space too long without a woman. Maybe the fact that his twin brother, Reid, had life mated to a woman after a lifetime of denying he ever would.

Reid had been the last of his four brothers to fall. Jarek was the only single cat-shifter prince left, and he liked it that way. As his upbringing would have him believe, life mating wasn't wise for the Var kind. Once life mated, it couldn't be undone. Cat-shifters lived a long time and passed that long life on to their life mates, aided by the same mystical power that guided them. But a lot could happen in the hundreds of years they lived. If a life mate died, the widower would be condemned to centuries of heartache. Many cat-shifters had died from such a lonely fate.

That's why Reid and Jarek had always planned on never falling in love. Of course, that was before Reid fell in love. Jarek did not wish to share his twin's fate. Sure, his brothers were happy in their marriages, happy and either expecting or with newborn sons. Jarek would like a son, someday. What man didn't? But to do so he only needed to half mate, and he could take many of those. What was the point of taking the risk of being with one woman? With so many beautiful women out there to sample, who wanted to choose just one and risk centuries of unhappiness?

His eyes roamed over the woman. Sacred cats! Why was he thinking about life mating right now? How in the galaxies did that train of thought come about? His body was talking sex and his mind was talking life mates?

It was like his father always warned him. *A woman has the potential to be the ruination of men and kingdoms. The only question is, my son, will you let one ruin you?*

King Attor might have been a warmonger, and Jarek might not have agreed with his father on much, but there were some things in which the man showed wisdom. Especially since striking out on his own into the galaxies, Jarek had heard tales of nations crumbling merely over the love of a woman. Every race had their stories of lost love, destroyed people and horrific deaths in the name of love. But, more importantly, he personally had seen some of the greatest men fall, namely his brothers. He didn't think it horrible that they had found love, and he liked his sisters-by-marriage, but his brothers would each give their own life, sacrifice everything, on behalf of their wives. He told himself that he wasn't keen on changing his ways, or worrying about someone else beyond his crew. It was ironic that, to have true love, you had to sacrifice part of yourself.

Jarek knew that he only told himself he didn't want a life mate to keep from admitting he, like every other warm-blooded creature, really did want such a fate. Only the greatest things could be achieved by having so much to lose. Without risk, there was no great reward. That settled it. He needed to, as Rick so delicately put it on many occasions, 'get his freak on'.

Whatever the bloody space nova that means.

Rick was addicted to twentieth century Earth culture, and he was always coming up with charming sayings to confuse them.

Jarek noticed neither of them was speaking, and the woman was staring at him, her brown eyes unwavering. Thinking of Rick, he growled. He had more pressing duties to tend to than sparring with this woman. Though fun, it would have to wait. First, he needed to get his ship repaired. Then he had to figure out a way to save his wayward friend. Word had come that Lucien and Viktor had retrieved the map though they weren't too forthcoming as to the 'how'. Jarek needed to see that map. He didn't have time for women.

"What are you?" the woman asked, staring at him. She crossed her arms over her chest. "Your face…you're a shifter, aren't you?"

Jarek lifted a hand to his cheek. His skin felt normal, but he realized from the tingling that he'd partially shifted while staring at her small breasts. Nails scraped across his skin, and he looked at his hands. Claws were retracting back into his fingers, and his palms were smudged with blood where he'd punctured himself. He balled his hands into fists to hide them and took a deep breath. It was too late. She'd seen it.

The woman's smell filled his nose. It was an exotic fragrance, mingled with the unmistakable scent of desire. No wonder his head was clouded and drifting. The woman was practically in heat. His shaft filled even more, instantly ready to do her body's silent bidding. But, looking at her eyes, her mind wasn't as welcoming to him. In fact, she looked a little frightened.

Sacred cats! He didn't need this distraction.

"I am captain of this ship," Jarek said, knowing full well he wasn't giving her the answer she desired. "And you, my lady cook, are my guest."

With that, he left her, locking her into the room. Until he had the ship well in hand, and the damage assessed, he didn't want the added worry of the pretty Lintianese flower on the loose.

"*Gaxìng jìandào nǐ!*" the woman yelled through the door. Jarek grinned. He really needed to upload her language, though by her hoarse yell it wasn't too hard to figure out that she was upset with him. "*Húndàn!*"

GUEST?

Mei frowned. Was that what they called prisoners? Guests? Shaking her head, she forced her eyes away from the locked door. She breathed heavily, caught between irritation and desire. To know she desired him only made her all the more irritated.

Why did he have to be so handsome? So thrilling and dangerous? She could've done without his subtle face shift. His brow had lengthened ever so slightly as his eyes had glowed with an eerie, animalistic gold. He'd looked like a beast, ready to pounce and take. The way her body heated, Mei had to admit she wasn't too averse to the getting taken part. Who was she fooling? She wasn't averse to the being pounced on part either.

Captain Jarek was well built and attractive in a very roguish sort of way. He'd changed his clothes and let down his hair. It fell in long dark waves to his waist, pulled up and back at the temples in braids to keep it out of his face. Now that she had looked at him fully, she noticed how dark his skin was, especially compared to her lighter complexion.

Black tattoos marked up one of his arms, the symmetrical pattern disappearing under his sleeve only to peek out of his collar by his neck. He was dressed in a loose white linen shirt, rolled at the sleeves, and tight black pants. His calf boots were polished to a high gleam. He scared her more than any man ever had. Which in turn only made her all the more annoyed with him and herself.

"So far they have acted honorably," she whispered, even though no one else was in the room to hear her. "Let's just hope that continues. But, for the time being, I'll just keep my mouth shut and see what I can discover."

Lying down on the bed, Mei stared at the metal ceiling.

"Computer, requesting security clearance," Mei said. The ship's mainframe didn't answer. If Haun had hit the ship with blasts of energy, it was quite possible they were adrift in space. Then why hadn't Haun come aboard? That was the whole point, disable the ship so it couldn't get away and then make demands while the ship was helpless and out of commission.

A sickening feeling curled in the pit of her

stomach. She grabbed a blanket and pulled it to her chest. Fear overwhelmed her as images of Haun's ship exploding invaded her imagination. The calm she felt moments before dissipated.

"Blessed ancestors, what have done?" Mei whispered. "Please keep Haun safe. I'll do whatever I have to, just keep my brother safe."

"Viktor, I need you to break the food simulator," Jarek ordered. He chuckled at the men's stunned expressions of utter horror. "It needs only to materialize uncooked ingredients."

"Have you gone mad?" Lucien protested, staring at his brother. "He'll never get around to fixing it again. We'll starve!"

Viktor leaned over the table and threw a piece of Qurilixen blue bread at him. The food was a favorite amongst the crew. Lochlann had introduced it to them the last time they were on the planet. "Ha ha, very funny."

They were in the commons, a lounge area equipped with a viewing screen, gaming tables, couches, and chairs. The men spent a lot of time there when they didn't want to be alone in their quarters. Lucien, Viktor, and Jackson leaned over the map with a hand held translator trying to read it. Dev watched quietly from behind, his arms crossed over his chest, and his eyes narrowed in concentration.

"No, our prisoner claims to be a royal chef," Jarek said. "So, let's see if she's telling the truth. Evan, I'll need you to watch her when she cooks. If she tries to poison us, you'll sense it. Dev, go to the cargo hold and crack open that wilderness kit we salvaged. There should be some cooking utensils in there somewhere that she can use. If anything, this will keep her busy while we do repairs."

Lucien chuckled. "Your sister-by-marriage would be so proud to hear you stole from the Human Intelligence Agency. I'm sorry, that we *salvaged* from the Human Intell—"

"First, *we* stole from them," Jarek corrected, giving a meaningful nod. His oldest brother, King Kirill was married to Ulyssa, an ex-HIA agent. She didn't talk about it to him too much, but from what he'd gathered, she had been one of their top agents. "Second, we didn't steal it from HIA. It was the Exploratory Science Commission and we simply salvaged what wasn't being used. Besides, ESC wasn't doing anything with it on Sintaz. It was just sitting there."

"Blessed stars! That planet was cold enough to steal the manhood from a libear," Jackson swore. "If I never go back there, I'll be a happy man."

"It's not our fault you accepted Rick's challenge," Lucien said. "You didn't have to run out of the ship naked into that snowdrift."

"Hey," Jackson protested, his eyes widening innocently. "He paid me twenty space credits."

"And you added new meaning to Rick's Old Earth term, blue balls," Lucien teased.

The men chuckled. Jarek looked down at the map, trying to memorize the lines as he listened to the others joke back and forth.

"But seriously here," Lucien said. "What if she can't cook? We'll all starve."

Viktor grimaced at his brother.

"Well, I guess that will make you our new chef," Jarek told Lucien, laughing as he glanced up for a brief second. The map was difficult to read. He didn't recognize the markings as they didn't resemble any map or chart he'd ever seen. It made sense. The Lintianese had isolated their culture for so long it was bound to be different and mysterious.

"We'll all be poisoned for sure," Jackson said dryly.

Viktor and Jackson groaned, grabbing their stomachs. Lucien rolled his eyes and shouted, "Hey, I'm not that bad!"

"You're not that good," Viktor teased. "Or so the women complain."

"At least leave it programmed to give out liquor," Jackson suggested.

"We should be studying the map," Dev reminded them sternly. He was the only one not joining in the ribbing.

"He's right." Jarek glanced up. "Any luck with the translator?"

"No," Jackson said, placing his hands on the table. "It doesn't recognize the symbols." He pointed at a long line that moved through squares. "I'm guessing this is a river of some sort by its curves in relation to everything else that's here, but without reading what it says, there is no way to be sure. These squares could be houses or property lines, farmland, or even...I don't know. These hieroglyphs are like none I've ever seen before."

The writing Jackson referred to was a series of square-like designs lined up from top to bottom.

"I picked up enough of her language from an old tracker, but I do not understand the writing," Dev said.

"Evan?" Jarek inquired, knowing that he was the most well-read of the group.

"I don't recognize it," he answered.

"We need someone to translate them for us," Jarek said, looking around the room meaningfully before turning in the direction of where their prisoner was locked away. "I just don't know if she's going to be willing to help us."

"Do we have a choice?" Evan asked.

"No." Jarek took a deep breath. "Unfortunately, we don't. Let's all upload her language as soon as possible. We should've done it before."

"There was no time before," Dev said. "There isn't much time now. We should be concentrating on repairs."

"We'll make time now. There really isn't a choice. Lucien, you go first. There isn't much you can do in communications until the systems are up and running. Evan, go with Viktor to break the food simulator, then bring the woman to the kitchen and see what you can find out. We need to know if we can trust her and right now it's the best thing we've got. The rest of us will get to work repairing the ship. I'm going to go see if Loch figured out where we are for sure."

"If I can access the computer," Jackson put forth, "I might be able to match these rivers to the landscape photographs stored in the logs. It might help us get an idea of what this thing says."

"Do it," Jarek ordered. "Right now that map and that woman are our best hope in getting Rick back."

"He owes us," Dev growled, even as his expression fell.

Jarek nodded in agreement. "Let's just hope we can save his butt in time to collect."

Mei absently threw food on the hot plate in front of her. The self-heating unit was used in camping, or so her guard told her. The stir fry was a simple dish, one she was more than trained to prepare. She doubted any of the pirate brutes would notice if she made the popular, unglamorous Lintianese dish instead of something a gourmet chef on her planet would create.

Mei laughed softly despite her distress. She doubted any of these brutes would know gourmet if they tasted it. They didn't seem to know a princess when they saw one.

The man guarding her, Evan, was polite. He tried to make conversation, but she didn't indulge him as she kept her attention on her task. Occasionally, she would speak to him in her own language. He didn't seem to understand it.

"How's it going in here?" Jarek's voice came from the dining hall door. "Smells interesting."

Mei's hand shook and she dropped too many minced peppers on the plate. They sizzled, sending a hot aroma up into the air. Instantly, the dining hall was filled with the spicy scent. She caught sight of Jarek from the corner of her eye, but didn't look at him directly as she stirred the food. Inside she shook, just like every time she was near him. The man definitely did something to her.

"She's not talking," Evan offered the captain.

"Mm, I like them silent," Jarek said, picking up one of the red peapods off the hot plate. He popped it in his mouth and chewed. Mei looked up at him and smiled. The pod was covered in the minced peppers she'd just dropped. Seconds later, it came flying out of his mouth as he coughed. "Sacred cats, Evan, she's trying to kill us!"

"Pepper too hot for you?" Mei teased, doing her best to sound meek. She pursed her lips and continued to stir.

"Hot?" Jarek let loose a long breath. "No, not hot. It tastes horrible."

Mei gasped in offense, looking down at the food. Horrible? Did he say it tasted horrible?

"You're no cook, *fea*," Jarek said. "Though, if

you were, it would explain why you are so tiny. With a diet like that, no wonder you don't eat."

Mei's jaw dropped and she stared at him. "I'm a good cook. I trained in the palace kitchens when I was a child."

Jarek smirked, glancing down from his impressive height. "Um, no. No, you're not, *fea*. It would explain why your people are so small as well. No doubt they can barely stomach the will to eat. It's a wonder they live at all."

"What?" Mei grabbed a warm peapod and thrust it into her mouth. It tasted fine to her, maybe a little too spicy hot, but fine. "There is nothing wrong with this."

"If you say so, *fea*." Jarek shrugged and walked around her. Mei spun on her heels, hands on hips, aware that he stood closer than was necessary. She tried to take a hurried step back, but her hip hit the table and she was trapped. Lifting her jaw, she met his eyes. It was a mistake. His gaze sparkled with the flecks of gold. Almost instantly, her insides melted and her heart beat picked up a few notches. His lips curled, drawing her eyes down as he spoke. "Do we have any of those Zigon paks left, Evan? Or maybe some of those ESC rations?"

"ESC rations?" Mei couldn't believe what she was hearing, as she was jolted to her senses. The Exploratory Science Commission had stopped on

Lintian to test farmland soil samples several years back. They thought the nutrients in their soil could help other planets whose farmland wasn't as thriving. Mei and her brother, Shen, had stayed in their camp for three days overseeing the operation while they collected their samples. The sealed packs of stew they provided for meals were some of the worst food she'd ever tasted. Years later, the thought of it still made her sick to her stomach.

And he thought her cooking was worse than that?

Stunned, she glanced over him. How in the seven galaxies did he get so large eating ESC rations?

"Excuse me? I'll have you know that I am the best chef on my planet," Mei lied.

"Poor planet," Jarek answered easily.

"Excuse me?" Mei demanded, unable to think of a better response.

"I said, I feel sorry for your planet if yours is the best cooking Lintian has to offer." Jarek grinned. It was a sexy, provocative smile. She wondered if he looked at her like that on purpose to disarm her. It was working. Her body was hot with desire and she couldn't stop staring into his dark eyes. He was tall and broad, dwarfing her in a way that was exciting. There was something very animalistic and potent in his bold ways, making her feel small and protected, yet vulnerable at the same time. He wasn't like the quiet men she had grown up around. There was life and vitality in every expression, a playfulness that gleamed in his gaze when he looked at her. The man was hardly a noble, that was for sure. His easy manner gave way to his lack of decorum.

You are not a princess here, Mei had to remind herself. *You are on the same level as him. That is why he treats you the way he does.*

Mei frowned. That wasn't necessarily true. She wasn't on the same level as him. She was a prisoner. If he knew she was a princess, he might not treat her any differently. Though, her value as a prisoner would go up. Would he ransom her to her family? Or just sell her and be done with it?

It's quite possible he's going to sell me anyway.

Was it better to tell him in hopes he'd ransom her back to her family?

Bide your time, Mei, bide your time. Keep your wits about you and try to discover what you're up against.

Her body tingled.

And keep your thighs closed as well!

"What happened to the ship that was following us?" she asked, her stomach knotted. Unable to keep moving, she stiffened, looking at Jarek as he answered.

"We escaped their attack by flying into a mage-feld," he answered.

Mei shivered. Her voice was soft, but she couldn't help it. Images of Haun dying floated in her head. She turned back to the food but didn't move as she stared at the sizzling pot. "And the other ship?"

"Unharmed," Jarek stated, his tone suddenly very stern and serious. Mei glanced up and nodded once. Relief curled inside of her at his words. She sensed he'd told the truth and felt as if a weight of stress and fear was lifted off her stomach. The devil-may-care attitude had faded from his expression only to quickly return.

"Where are the other women?" she asked, turning back to her food. If he didn't want it there'd just be more for her. Let him have his disgusting ESC rations.

Jarek shared a look with Evan and laughed.

"You find kidnapping us amusing, *chûnrén?*"

"Ah, *fea*, you break my heart. At least get to know me first before you think me foolish." Jarek winked.

Mei paled. He understood her. "I know all I want to know about you, captain. And my name is Mei."

"Mei," Jarek repeated softly, a strange look on his face as he looked at her. If she didn't know better she would've thought he was enamored of her. "So, Mei, are those women friends of yours?"

"Yes," she lied. "And I want to assure their safety. I demand you let me see them."

"Demand?" He laughed, shaking his head in amusement. "Mei, you remember Dev don't you?"

The big red guy came out from behind the door as if he'd been standing guard all along. Mei shivered. She'd thought of running and was glad she'd decided against it. Dev lifted his jaw. He was undoubtedly their most fearsome warrior.

"He's going to keep an eye on you," Jarek said, motioning Evan to follow. Giving his cocky grin, he whispered to her. "Be good, *fea*. Don't get into any trouble and don't poison my crew."

Mei made a face at the captain. Jarek grinned, and the look shot through her like lightning. Just wonderful. Now her body was moist as well as aroused. It took all her effort not to wiggle in frustration. The last thing she needed was to have burning desires for her arrogant captor.

"Dev," Jarek said, as he and Evan stepped out, "you know what to do with her if she misbehaves."

Dev nodded once. Mei shivered, wondering just what that punishment would be. She quickly turned back to cooking, doing her best to ignore her giant bodyguard as she silently cursed the pirate captain.

JAREK STRODE from the dining hall. He couldn't help the grin that spread over his face. The woman was entertaining, he'd give her that—so easy to tease. There was just something about her, something that made him want to trust her even though he knew she was lying to him. There was a subtle change in her smell when she lied, like when she had said she was a cook. The fragrance was faint, but he was so in tune with her that he had caught it easily.

When they were down the corridor, far away from hearing distance, Evan said, "You did well taking her off guard by insulting her cooking. It was the first clear read I got from her. She is very disciplined. I can't tell if it's because she suspects me reading her, or if she is always so guarded. I can barely even feel fear."

"Maybe she doesn't fear us," Jarek said.

"Perhaps." Evan stopped walking and glanced back. "She has no problem lying to us, though."

"Claiming to know Viktor and Lucien," Jarek answered, knowing that was what Evan was speaking of. There was no way Mei knew the two men. She was bluffing.

"Yes. And about being a chef. Was her food that bad?"

"No," Jarek chuckled. "It was actually quite good. It was all I could do to keep my stomach from growling for more."

Evan smiled.

"But, that woman is no chef. I'd bet my life on it. I could smell her lie when she said it, same as when she said she knew Vik and Lucien." Jarek sighed. "She's nobility, or at least has some sort of elected power. That man she was with was probably a brother or husband."

"You're certain?"

"Oh yeah. She has that attitude about her. Servants don't demand, don't look at people the way she does. That kind of thing is bred into a person. She's too regal in her movements."

"I agree. But then why did she come after us?"

"Perhaps it was to save the two women." Jarek swallowed. *Or to escape her duty and position.*

He knew all about escaping his princely title. It's why he'd cultivated his easy demeanor so that no one could tell what he was unless he wanted them to.

"Unfortunately, I can't get a good enough read on her to recommend showing her the map. I might be able to sense her lie if she tried to mislead us, but I can't be certain of it."

Jarek took a deep breath. "What do you recommend?"

"Time. She's different when you're in the room. You know I hate revealing what I read, but…"

"Rick's life is on the line. Time is something we don't really have." Jarek placed his hand on Evan's arm.

"I know."

"What did you sense?" Jarek wanted to shake the man, desperate to hear what he had learned about the woman.

"She's not immune to your charms. You confuse her, but you also interest her. She didn't have that reaction to me, or to Dev. It was unique when you walked into the room. I think she likes you. A lot."

Jarek grinned. How could he not? Evan's words boosted his male vanity greatly.

"I don't say this because I want you to take advantage of her," Evan put forth sternly, pointing at Jarek in warning, "but out of necessity. Out of any of us, she might come to trust you the soonest. I will continue to study her. With time, I will learn more. But if she were to develop an attachment to the crew, to..." Evan gave him a meaningful look.

"To me," Jarek finished. Evan was telling him to seduce her, to make her love him. His gut tightened. "I hate lying to her like that. I'm not so cold that I'd pretend to love when it's not there."

"I know, I hate it too." Evan's smile was sad. "There is a fine line between lust and love, but if you're careful maybe you can walk it."

Jarek knew Evan never used his gift to harm others. He often went out of his way not to reveal what he knew, unless it was to judge someone's intent against the crew. He could see by the look on his friend's face that it was hurting him to even suggest this course of action. Though, if Evan said it, he truly believed it was the only course for them to take. It wasn't as if Rick had left them with too many options.

"I just wish we knew if he was alive or not," Jarek sighed.

"If anyone can charm a kidnapper, it's Rick."

"This is our only option, isn't it?" Jarek glanced back down the corridor to where Mei was in the dining hall. It's not as if it would be hard to force himself to bed her. In fact, his body was more than willing to jump into it. He closed his eyes briefly, picturing her. She had her long, gorgeous hair down, but she still wore the gown she'd arrived in. The silky locks made him want to run his fingers through them, just as her smooth skin beckoned his hands. There were many things he'd like to do to her. He reined his imagination in.

"I'm afraid so," Evan agreed, frowning. "You have any ideas on how you're going to do it?"

"Seduction is the last thing I need help with." Jarek stretched his arms over his head. Part of him liked the idea of seducing Mei. The other part of him still liked the idea but was sorry that it would come about with such deceit. He hated the plan of purposefully breaking a woman's heart for that was surely what would happen if Mei fell in love with him. Usually, he was honest about that fact from the beginning. With her, he couldn't risk it. The more she cared about the fate of his crew, of him, the more willing she'd be to help them. It was this or risk losing their friend forever.

"Rick would sacrifice for us," Evan said.

Jarek knew the man was picking up on his emotions. He nodded once in agreement and understanding.

"People do mend from a broken heart," Evan whispered. "Trust me. In time, she will heal."

"Not all people." Jarek took a deep breath. "But there is no cure for death if we don't find Rick. I'll do it. I'll seduce her tonight. It'll be the fastest love story in history."

MEI FROWNED across the table at Jarek. He ate her food with relish, as did everyone else—Dev, Evan, Lochlann, and Jackson. Why in the world was the pirate captain enjoying the meal if it was so horrible? He looked at her, grinning impishly at her as he chewed.

Her heart leaped around in her chest, and her stomach fluttered as if the wings of the *qizajian* beat inside her. The winged creatures were often seen in the gardens of the Zhang palace. Their bodies were small compared to their large black wings. What made them sacred was the fact that their wings formed the shape of the Old Earth character '7'. Seven was an unlucky number. It meant death. Her people believed to kill them was to bring death and so they were allowed free reign over the palace.

But, just like everything, the *qizajian* were necessary to the life of the garden. Life and death, two necessary opposites. Without one, there could be no other.

She couldn't help but recognize the comparison of the *qizajian* and the feelings inside her. If she killed her feelings for Captain Jarek, did she risk hurting part of herself?

Don't be foolish and sentimental. Of course, I should deny feeling anything for him. What about Lok? What about great-grandmother's prediction? I am meant to marry Lok. To even mess with Captain Jarek is to mess with fate.

However, a tiny voice whispered as if brought up from the heating of her lower stomach, *you are not betrothed to him yet. You are free to enjoy the attentions of other men. Lok has not proposed. Only fate has been laid out. Perhaps taking the pirate as a lover is fate's way of apologizing for the necessity of taking Prince Lok. Perhaps he is fate's gift.*

Wasn't that why she flew through the air to fight the pirates? She wanted a last adventure before marriage. There was no doubt in her mind that she was meant to marry Lok. However, no moment of intimacy had passed between them. And, if fate had her marrying the Song prince, surely that meant that she would arrive safely back on her planet. As soon as she arrived there, would she be engaged to him? Would something happen in her absence to make their marriage a necessity? Could Lok be proposing marriage to her father even now, providing she was returned unharmed? Would that proposal be out of a sense of guilt because she was kidnaped going after their *pu ren*? Prince Lok hadn't seemed interested in her, but what if she'd misread him? What if she'd wanted it not to happen so badly that she'd ignored all the signs of his attraction?

Was Jarek her last chance at tasting freedom?

Would her mind ever stop with all the questions?

Mei shivered at her new course of thought, unsure if she was just making excuses to justify her attraction to the man. Nothing more could ever come between them, but he was a man and seducing him would be very easy. If the looks he gave her weren't any indication, the stiff erection he'd gotten earlier in her presence was. He wanted her, maybe as badly as she wanted him. Chewing thoughtfully, she clamped her legs together. Jarek's gaze jerked to hers, suddenly serious. His nostrils flared slightly as if he could smell her sudden burst of longing. One of the men said something, drawing his attention back, but she couldn't understand them through the blood rushing in her head. Mei took a hurried bite, doing her best to hide her reaction.

Those thoughts led to more, and she again forgot to eat as she stared at Jarek's mouth. It moved slowly, taking small bites of the meal. What kind of lover would he be? Bold and wild like a pirate's ways? She squirmed in her seat. His mouth stopped, and his nostrils flared once more as desire ran rampant inside her. It was as if her body had just been waiting for permission to want him and, now that it had, it was going to take full advantage, making sure she didn't change her mind.

"Out," Jarek barked. The men turned to him in mid-conversation in stunned surprise. Mei didn't even hear their response, only their grumbling protests. They looked at Jarek, not moving. "I said out. Leave us. Now."

The men instantly stood, taking their plates with them as they left the dining hall. The low murmur of their voices followed them, growing quieter the further away they got.

Jarek breathed heavily. Mei felt the animalistic power in him, the *dòngwù*, the beast waiting to get out. His untamed ways excited her. Slowly, he stood. Her eyes traveled down his tight, thick body to the prominent erection bulging against his pants. He crossed over to the dining hall door and ran his hand over the sensor, shutting it. The clank of metal against metal seemed soft compared to the heartbeat echoing in her head.

He stood several steps away. Mei rose to her feet, swallowing as she tried to keep herself from leaping on him. It was a strange feeling. The more she desired him, the more heated she became, the more he seemed to emit some sort of powerful pheromone she couldn't resist. The smell of food disappeared, replaced by the heady scent of man.

No one will ever know my secret. This pirate will be my secret.

Mei took a deep breath. Every nerve she had focused on him. Her eyes traveled his frame. He was so big in size compared to the lovers she'd had. The thought thrilled her. She had wanted an adventure, and here he was.

Part of her felt bad for using him in such a way, but surely he wouldn't get too attached. He was a pirate after all. They were used to taking what they wanted. Selfish motivation would drive him to her bed, and when the time came, it would take him out of it. There was no risk in this for either of them. And, if he did come to enjoy her company just enough, perhaps he'd take her home in exchange for a clean getaway. The plan had merit. Mei gave a slow grin, feeling very wicked and naughty. The plan included her getting the very handsome Captain Jarek into her bed.

She glanced around the room. Bowls of food were still on the table, what was left of her cooking.

Or would that be, getting the very handsome Captain Jarek into her 'dining hall'?

"Tell me, captain," Mei said, giving him a seductively modest look from beneath her lashes as she lifted her hand to the thick belt at her waist. With a single pull, she untied it. The embroidered silk slithered to the floor, landing at her feet. The gown she wore loosened from her waist, but still covered her fully. "Is it true what they say about space pirates?"

Jarek took a slow step forward, his eyes leisurely looking her over. They lingered on her hips and breasts, as he licked the corner of his mouth. "What is it they say?"

"That you have insatiable appetites for all things—food, thievery, women." Mei wiggled her shoulders, causing the gown to fall. It exposed her collarbone to him but did not drop beneath her breasts. Jarek's breath caught, as he stared at her neck. A tremor worked its way over her at his hot look. The golden flecks came back to his eyes, burning with desire. Her thighs clamped as her body stiffened. Anticipation made her rigid as she kept herself back from him.

"Are you asking to find out?" A low growl had taken over his words. He was breathing as hard as she, the sound harsh. He licked his lips, drawing her eyes to their firmness. "Or are you looking to negotiate?"

"You know I want my freedom." Mei didn't bother to lie. "And I'm willing to be very good in exchange for it."

Jarek's breath caught, and he seemed to struggle to concentrate on her soft words. Mei purposefully kept her manner meek and mild. Big, strong men always liked meek women. It made them feel powerful, and she had no problem using his male vanity to manipulate him.

"That isn't necessary," Jarek answered after some length. He took a deep breath and then another. Mei was too stunned to talk. Was he rejecting her? It was clear that he wanted her. Why in the world wasn't he kissing her right now? "You don't...I should...Dev will show you to your quarters."

Jarek spun on his heels, leaving her to stare after him as he opened the door and walked out. Mei didn't move. Did a pirate, a man who by design had no morals, just reject her?

She stood so long that Dev was in the doorway looking at her by the time she shook herself from her stupor. As regally as she could muster, she picked up her belt and hurriedly tied it around her waist. How could he do this to her? How could

Jarek reject her when it was clear he didn't want to? And, more puzzling was, why?

"My lady?" Dev said. "I'm to take you to your quarters."

Anger built inside her as she nodded. Rage was easier than the hurt of rejection. Stiffly, she allowed Dev to lead her back to her room.

13

JAREK TOOK a deep breath and then another. It was late, but they were making steady progress on the ship repairs. The shockwaves from the Lintianese spacecraft had fried many of their circuits, but Dev was able to dig up replacements for most of the damaged parts out of their cargo hold.

"Good thing we found that somewhat abandoned ESC shipment," was all Dev said as he handed the parts over.

The first thing to repair had been the life support systems. Once they were online and tested, the crew worked on the engine. Jackson wasn't having any luck matching the Lintianese map Viktor and Lucien had stolen, but at least they knew where they were. Lochlann was able to find their current location in the star charts. Unfortunately, they were adrift in space, far away from any ready port. Until they could risk turning on the thrusters without burning off the oxygen in the air supply, they were almost completely helpless.

"Bloody nova," Jackson swore, sitting back. He threw a tool on the ground. It clanked against the metal floor, skidding across the small engine room. "I hate this stupid hunk of metal ship!"

Jackson kicked the wall several times, growling loudly each time his foot bashed metal before storming out. When he had gone, the rest of them laughed. Though, truth be told, they all felt the man's frustration. After a vigorous walk and maybe a drink, Jackson would come back and get to work.

"So," Jarek said to lighten the mood and to get his mind off of Mei… Mei, lying all alone in her room. Mei, dropping her belt in the dining hall. Mei's dark, exotic eyes glancing up at him through her thick lashes. "Uh-hem, so Vik, Lucien?"

"Yeah, cap?" they said in unison.

"How did you get the map?" Jarek asked, pretending to study his laser wrench carefully.

Viktor and Lucien shared a look.

"Ah, come on guys, you're not ashamed of anything you had to do, are you?" Evan teased. "We'll understand that you didn't enjoy it, and it was all in the name of friendship."

"Yeah," Jackson added from the door, holding a

red bottle of Qurilixian liquor that Jarek and Lochlann had stocked the last time they were home. He looked as if he'd never thrown the tirade. "How come your clothes were all disheveled?"

Jarek set down his laser as Jackson handed him the opened bottle. He took a quick drink. The liquor was thick and burned as it went down. He wiped his lip on the back of his hand and gave it to Dev, who took a swig and passed it over Viktor's head to Evan.

"Nothing happened," Viktor said, his eyes following the bottle.

"We saw the map, and we took it," Lucien added.

"In and out, really simple." Viktor started to reach for the bottle, but it was passed by him again.

"In and out, eh?" Jackson teased.

The men laughed, and the bottle was passed back around to everyone but the two brothers.

"Come on, give us a drink," Viktor said. "You should be thanking us. We were the ones that risked our necks by going into the Lintianese palace. It was dangerous in there, and you all know it."

"Are you sure it was your necks you were risking?" Jarek teased. He finally passed the bottle to Viktor.

"Ha ha, very funny, space cadets," Viktor

mumbled, before drinking and passing to his brother.

"You're the one who said in and out," Lucien laughed. "I don't remember any such thing. Though, I do recall a time when I was looking for the map and you—"

"Eh!" Viktor frowned and swiped the bottle before Lucien could have any.

Jarek laughed with the others. It was all good-natured teasing.

"It's getting late," Jarek said. "Let's work in shifts."

"If you leave the bottle of rum, I'll go first," Lochlann said.

Jarek nodded.

"I'll stay," Viktor offered. "I'm not really tired."

"Me too," Lucien added. "I want to check out the communications system just in case we find ourselves stranded."

"Good idea," Jarek agreed. Dev was the only one who kept working without comment. "The rest of you, go and get some sleep. We'll work in four-hour shifts."

"What about you, captain?" Jackson asked, slowly running a dirty rag over a pipe he'd been working on.

"What about me?" Jarek asked.

"You going to, ah, go rest?" As he said the last two words, Lucien wagged his eyebrows.

"Yeah, captain, are you going to check on the prisoner?" Lochlann nudged Evan in the arm. He grinned mischievously, trying to hold back laughter.

"She's not a prisoner," Jarek denied. "We rescued her."

"Mm-hmm," Viktor said unconvinced.

"Dev, you saw it. She practically attacked me to get away from that man." Jarek motioned to Dev for help.

"Looked like she was trying to fight you," Dev said, ever stoic. He stopped working to look up. "To me, that is."

"You all are impossible," Jarek grumbled. "I'm going to bed." At the laughs, he added, "Alone."

"That's nothing to be bragging about." Jackson patted him on the arm as he joined him. "I'll sleep in the cockpit with my ears open, just in case we get any company."

Jarek growled mockingly at their knowing looks, letting the tiger he could become enter his voice, and shook his head. "Four hours and then we switch. Send someone around if everyone doesn't get up. Without the computer, we can't set the alarms."

As he went toward the engine room door, Evan joined them. They walked in silence through the corridor until Jackson veered off toward the cockpit.

"I hope you have a plan," Evan said.

"I do," Jarek lied. He thought of Mei, still smelling her desire for him lingering in his memory. The wild cat in him wanted to shift, go after her and lay claim. The urge was strong, too strong for his liking.

"That was almost convincing," Evan said. "The slow courting is nice and all, but we don't have the time. Maybe you should go and see if she needs anything. Make sure she's warm enough, safe enough."

Jarek chuckled softly though he didn't feel amused. Every nerve burned to possess her, to make her his. That scared him. The passion was too much, too hot. With every blink, he saw her long hair flowing about her slender body. She was so delicate, so tiny. Her face was so beautiful, exotically so. Even her smell appeared sweeter than other women he had known. In all his sixty- two years, he'd never reacted so strongly.

"Fine. I'll go to her. If you truly think that is best." Jarek wondered why he was hesitating.

"By the way you were looking at each other over dinner..." Evan paused, grinning. "Let's just say a person doesn't have to be telepathic to figure out what's going on between you two. I was surprised you didn't finish what was there."

"Of course I desire her. She's beautiful." Jarek motioned his hand in dismissal as if it was no big deal.

"All right," Evan agreed.

"It's been a while since we had leisure time," he continued.

"Mm-hmm. It's been a bit."

"And the fact that she desires me is to be understood. I do not lack in charm. Many women find me attractive."

"Okay."

"Oh, Sacred cats! Shut your mouth, Evan. I wish to hear no more of your nonsense." Jarek walked faster.

Accursed telepath! Thinks he knows everything.

Jarek suddenly stopped, finding himself at Mei's door. He lifted his hand toward the scanner, hesitated, took a deep breath and then lowered it again. Staring at the rigid steel door, he didn't move. He let his senses shift and enhance so he could sense her beyond the metal. Imagination helped as he pictured her resting on the bed, her dark hair fanned out around her face, her eyes closed, those dark lashes against her cheeks.

Her smell wrapped around his senses. It called to him. He again lifted his hand. One peek to make sure she was all right was all he needed. Just to make sure she didn't require anything. Running his hand over the sensor, he waited for the door to slide open. His eyes changed with the power of the cat-shifter, and they instantly went to the bed.

An empty mattress was all he saw before a fist swung for his face. It smacked his nose. The blow was hard, taking him off guard. He'd been so focused on keeping his desires at bay, that he'd dropped his defenses. Falling back, he grunted as a knee hit his gut. He smelled Mei without seeing her. She struck his back, knocking him over to the floor with surprising force.

Jarek growled as he heard her run down the corridor. Her steps were light, but he detected her direction easily. Leaping to his feet, he ran after her.

"Mei," he said harshly, rubbing his jaw. Her punch had hurt. He was impressed.

"Stay away from me, pirate," he heard her whisper. Suddenly, her footfalls stopped. Jarek ran faster, sure he was about to reach her.

Frowning when he didn't immediately catch up to her, he stopped, sniffing around. He hadn't heard any of the doors lift. Catching the faintest trace, he looked up. One of the panels was removed from the top of the corridor. Wires hung out. It would be a tight fit, but Mei was tiny. Jumping, he grabbed the edge and pulled his weight up so he could look down it. The narrow space was dark, but his eyesight cut easily through the blackness. There was no trace of Mei, except for her scent. She'd jumped up into the corridor ceiling and scurried away. Since he was too big to fit up there, he'd never explored that part of his ship. Lucien and Viktor might be the only guys he could send after her, but he needed them to work on repairs.

Angry, he slowly lowered his body down to the corridor floor. Mei could be anywhere on the ship and, unfortunately, he couldn't access the system to find her. Well, if she wanted to sleep on cold metal, tangled in wires, he would let her.

It's not as if she can go anywhere.

Rubbing his sore jaw, he went back to the engine room. After telling the guys to watch what they said because Mei was on the loose, he took the map from Jackson and went back to his own quarters. Sure, he could spend the entire night searching for her, but he had a feeling it would do little good. He also didn't sense a killer in her, so there would be no harm to his crew. Besides, they could handle themselves. Touching his face, he chuckled. Maybe he should worry about it, just a little.

14

MEI GRUNTED, biting her lip as she tried to wiggle through a tight spot in the ductwork along the corridor ceiling. Wires, pipes, circuits, computer access panels and a few things she was sure they'd just stored up in the dusty place, crowded her in. Sneezing, she cursed silently as she paused to make sure no one had heard her.

Men. Couldn't they be bothered to get the ship cleaned? They had droids for this sort of thing. It's a surprise this hunk of tin flies at all with the way they take care of it.

Seeing a broken cleaning droid through a thin band of light coming from below, she chuckled. It seemed the dust was too much for even it to handle. She pushed the little unit out of her way and crawled forward on her stomach. The fit might be tight, but she had to laugh as she thought of how perfect it was. There was no way Jarek was coming up after her. Though, it would be funny to watch him get stuck trying.

Hearing clanking, she followed the sounds. A soft murmur of voices grew steadily. It was the crew. Peeking through a seam in the ceiling, she saw a blur of movement followed by laughter.

There was more clanking and the sound of lasers being used. She adjusted her weight, tilting her head back and forth to try and get a better view. It was no use. She couldn't make out more than the blur of colors as the men moved past her line of vision. Mei tried to breathe slowly through her nose, so she didn't inhale too much dust.

"I'm sure Rick's fine," one of the men said.

"There's nothing we can do right now anyway," another answered.

Mei leaned closer, turning her head to see through the seam. The voices sounded familiar, but they were too foreign for her to make out who was who.

"Do you think that woman will be all right crawling around up there?"

Mei pressed her ear to metal, listening very closely.

"Sure she will, Evan. There's nothing up there but wires."

"Jarek didn't seem worried."

"Give me that bottle."

"Hey, I wasn't done with that."

A round of laughter followed by a loud bang, as if someone had thrown a tool, echoed from below.

"Lochlann figure out where we are yet?"

So far, Jarek hadn't spoken. By the way someone had said his name, she guessed he wasn't part of the group. A flash of red skin passed her view, and she knew it was Dev.

"Somewhere along the X, that's all I've heard."

"Yeah," there was a pause and the sound of a bottle being set down. "We're adrift in the stars."

"Nothing in sight."

Mei frowned. Her stomach knotted. Did these pirates get them lost? Were they all going to die floating around in space like some kind of galactic waste?

"No one will ever know to look for us here."

They sounded worried. She waited, breath held.

"Sta-a-a-rs all 'round us," one of the men broke into song. His voice wasn't bad though the tone of the music was strange to her ears.

"My galactic playma-a-a-a-a-te and me," the others joined in, a slightly frightening off-key melody, as they sang about stars and night and the loving arms of well-endowed prostitutes.

Mei suppressed a laugh, covering her fingers

over her mouth, even as a smile crossed over her face. Laying her head down, she just listened to them. They didn't seem like a bad bunch of guys. She didn't detect any malice in them. Strange, but if she hadn't seen them with her own eyes, she wouldn't have taken them for pirates.

As the song ended, they laughed.

"Ah, I miss Ruby. The way she danced! Ow! Ow-ooo!"

"Mm, Topaz, my dark sugar coated goddess of love."

"Diamond, she had eyes like stars and the body of a…*mmm.*"

"Didn't you hear, Vik? Diamond got married. Some guy named Liam. He's her bodyguard now and won't let me within fifty feet of her."

"No, say it isn't so," the one they called Vik exclaimed.

"I'd like to guard that body. Talk about a lucky man. I proposed to all three of them. They all said no."

"Ah, I'm sure you were just too much man for them, Jackson."

"Don't talk about those women," Dev's voice interrupted. Now his she recognized. "You'll only depress yourselves and I'll have to listen to you whine all night about how you don't have any women."

"Hey, don't tell, man. We have a tough image to uphold," Vik answered.

Again there was laughter.

"You wouldn't know true love if it hit you," Dev grumbled.

"She did hit me once," Vik said. "Had a monster of a right hook. Mm, she was gorgeous."

A loud snort sounded.

"Whoa, someone is touchy? Need a little action, Dev?"

"A little..." A throat cleared. "Uh-hem. Action of the high skies?"

Laughter sounded.

"Ah, not that one again," Dev protested, his voice loud and pleading.

"What's wrong, Dev?" Vik cried. "Don't you like to sing?"

"I like silence much better," Dev answered, sounding brusque.

The men instantly broke out into a lively, robust song.

"Our birth was a hard one, or so we've been told, our mothers were harlots our fathers out cold. The doctor was drunk, lads, the bartender did pour, as we shot out with the thunder and came with a roar."

Mei bit the back of her hand to keep from laughing. The song was atrocious, worse than the first. She'd never heard anything like it. She'd never heard men like these. Their vigorous singing continued.

"Up from the trenches of Ole Skull and Bones, we swabbed that cold deck and that black how it shone. The cap'n was surly, lads, and the crew stank a lot, as each one grew famous down to the last shot.

"No dry land for us, we pay our due to the sky, and so we shall e'er 'til the day we do die. No tears for a pirate, lads, for shed them we not. Our life we do live for that's what we got.

"And we sail the high skies, looking for gold, looking for treasures that never grow old. The wind in our sails, lads, the stars at our feet, as we plunder for women, thick brown, and good mead."

A round of laughter broke out as the song ended. Mei pushed up on her hands, crawling backward the way she'd come. She had a ship to explore before showing herself again, and she had those kidnaped women to find. They began their pirating song once more, much to Dev's grumbling. She knew by the way they slurred that they had to be far into their cups. The clanking became louder as they worked.

Wonderful, she thought, *lost in space with a group of drunken pirates. Not even great-grandmother, with all her afterlife wisdom, could have predicted this.*

15

Jarek tensed but didn't open his eyes. A noise had jerked him from sleep, not that he'd been sleeping that well to begin with. He'd been dreaming of Mei, of making love to her. His shaft was hard, needy, so full it felt like it would burst. Why hadn't he taken her offer in the dining hall? If he had just given her what she'd wanted there and then, without suddenly worrying that he wanted her too much, his body wouldn't ache so badly.

Desired her too much.

He took a deep breath. Now, alone and deprived in his dark quarters, it sounded foolish.

He listened to his room, mentally traveling over the wide space. He had the captain's quarters, the largest sleeping chambers on the ship. Thick, blue carpet covered the metal floor, which muffled sounds. In the corner was a small, round table with a computer built into the dark wood base. Any game imaginable could be played on it. Two thick-cushioned chairs were by the table. Their dark blue matched the floor.

There was a cream colored couch with computer controls in the arms and a viewing screen he'd installed especially so he could watch Old Earth transmissions. Most of what the ship stored was Old Earth documentaries on the acts of mating, thanks to Viktor sharing his great collection. They were a ship favorite. However, there were also plenty of action films. Most of them were funny, but they had big fiery explosions and creative fights that made them pleasurable to watch. He especially liked the ones where the flying humans danced on the tree tops while fighting in the limbs, leaping about. He'd never met a humanoid with such a graceful ability, but the way the Lintianese moved came close.

Not detecting anything with the viewing screen, he mentally drew his attention across to the other side. His bed was along a wall. It retracted to make more space, not that it was really needed. A large decontaminator with seats and the door was opposite the couch. Jarek couldn't sense anything there either.

Then, the faintest trace of Mei drifted over

him. She was near. He stretched out his senses, not moving as he felt for her. She was above him, in the ceiling. Jarek slept naked by habit and adjusted his legs as if in sleep. He pulled the covers down his chest to just above his ever-stiffening erection.

He was so focused, he heard her breath catch and then quicken. She was spying on him. Jarek forced himself to stay calm when every nerve was tense with lust. Moaning lightly, he drew the sheet down, so the tip of his arousal was exposed. It took all his energy not to touch himself. Jarek bent his knees, letting them fall open. It was erotic, knowing she watched him, knowing what he did turned her on even more than it did him.

A small sound, like a ceiling panel being adjusted caught his attention. He detected the air stirring with movement. Was she coming into his room?

Mei dropped lightly to the floor. He waited, sensing her hesitance, a trace of her fear. She wasn't leaving.

Suddenly, the tension coiled within him sprung, causing him to strike out like a *givre*. He saw something sharp and metallic in her hand, outlined by the dim light from his wall panel. Grabbing her wrist, he blocked off any attack. It wasn't necessary. Her hand was relaxed, and the surprise of his assault caused her to drop a ragged piece of metal.

Whatever her intent had been in coming to his room, she'd not gone through with the idea. Her body was too off guard, and she was too surprised to be in an offensive fighting mode.

Mei's rounded eyes met his as he stood next to the bed. The air was warm, and he felt the heat centering between his thighs. She looked down, her gaze stopping on his thick erection. He followed her eyes. Only her clothing stood between them. The knowledge was too much.

Jarek jerked her forward by the wrist he had captured. Her small body fit against him, and he automatically flexed his erection into her. The softness of her felt good, combined with the silk of her clothing. He could smell the dust on her from crawling around the ship's ceiling.

Reaching for her face, he cupped her jaw only to drag her lips roughly forward as he leaned down to kiss her. She gasped, but let his tongue plummet into her willing mouth. Jarek devoured her with that kiss, trying to take all of her in. He breathed her air, felt her body's every subtle movement as she accepted what was between them.

Thoughts of Rick, of making her fall in love with him, left him. He was in the moment, trapped by Mei's spell. Whoever she was, in this moment, she was his. All his.

The soft locks of her hair tangled in his fingers. He thrust along the silk, liking the way it slid between their bodies. His hands found her shoulders, gliding easily over her silk covered back to her nice, round ass. Squeezing it, he lifted her up slightly before putting her back down. She was so light, he couldn't resist doing it again and again, as he lifted her up and down along his harder frame. The light sound of her playful laugh washed over him.

Soon, the silk against his flesh wasn't enough. He needed to feel her naked skin. Mei made a soft purring sound, touching his hair, his neck, and his shoulders. She whispered to him, but he couldn't concentrate enough to understand her language. Jarek didn't need to understand. He knew she spoke sultry words of passion and desire. He growled in response.

Eagerly, he pulled up her silk gown. She was naked beneath, and he was glad for it. The shoulder of the dress fell aside, exposing one small breast. He growled in the back of his throat, beyond words of any kind. Animal instinct took over completely.

Grabbing her hips, he lifted her up. Mei wrapped her arms around his neck, keeping their kiss deep. Her legs found a hold along his waist as her moist slit pressed tightly to his stomach. She wiggled against him. He didn't bother lying down. The need was too urgent.

Guiding her hips, he drew her along his arousal. He lifted her up and down, letting her body's moisture wet him. She gasped, arching back. Jarek instantly dropped his face to her exposed breast, sucking it between his lips. She tasted sweet and smelled even better. He liked the way her breast filled his mouth.

Jarek thrust, pulling her down onto his ready shaft. Just as he imagined, her body was tight, clinging erotically to him as he stretched her to fit. The wet cream of her was heavenly as he eased in and out, working against her, spreading her wider, making her take him all in.

Mei made a weak sound, gasping for breath, but she didn't pull off as she moved with his thrusts. Jarek pushed his heels into the floor, bending his knees slightly as he moved his hips in little circles.

Mei pressed into his chest. Caught off guard, he fell back onto the bed. She landed on him, his shaft embedding deeply into her with the impact of the fall.

Jarek liked the new position. Mei clawed his skin, wiggling on top of him in deep circles. He felt her muscles contracting along him, squeezing him tight. Taking her hips, he drew his hands along her silk covered waist, using the disheveled gown to caress her skin. He found her breasts, one with flesh, the other with silk, and massaged them, budding the tight nipples even more.

Mei moved gracefully as she kept her own rhythm. Jarek just let her have her way, shifting his eyes so he could watch the erotic show. The woman rode him, her lips parted, her lids heavy. She groaned passionately as she worked faster and faster. The silk of her gown entranced him, the way it wrapped and clung to her body as she practically danced above him.

He slid his thighs open, forcing her legs wider apart. Mei groaned, a low, throaty sound of pleasure and approval. The noise she made enthralled him. Her body continued to move gracefully as she leaned back and reached behind her.

The visual was too much. Jarek felt himself close to coming. He gripped her narrow hips tightly and tried to control her movements. Her small hand slipped onto his balls, massaging them. He tensed, seconds away from spilling his seed. The feeling of eruption was almost painful as it tightened his gut and swelled his balls. His body shook, he got ready, and then she pulled firmly down on his balls. The gesture stopped the flow of his seed as he orgasmed. Jarek grunted, his arousal still hard as a rock as he shook with a partial release.

"Too soon," she whispered, still holding his

balls as she wiggled more. It was divine torture. "I will show you how to go longer, to take more, to conserve your energies."

Numbly, completely captivated, he nodded his head in agreement. In that moment, he'd agree to anything she commanded. Mei seemed to understand this because a small catlike smile curled the side of her mouth. She lifted above him, raising her hands up as she used her thighs to push up and down.

A low throaty laugh left her and she grinned down at him, proud of what she had done. "I like it when your eyes glow like that, *qin ài de.* You're trying to hide yourself from me, your shifter self."

Jarek grunted, caught between the need to claim her with his seed and the hold she had on him, controlling him with the subtle shifting of her muscles.

"What kind?" Mei demanded, not moving.

"Cat," he gasped, unable to lie in that moment. At the word, he felt her body wetting him more. She liked it. The knowledge made it difficult to concentrate. She had him right where she wanted him, and they both knew it.

The cat-shifters were sexual creatures, but to play with the beast, to encourage the very nature of the predator could lead to uncontrollable passion. He'd be mindless, unable to stop once he started.

Jarek tried to regain control, but Mei seemed to have something else in mind.

"Do you want to see?" he whispered. He would never take her in his completely shifted form, but he could let parts of the creature out—fangs, claws, voice, and eyes. By the way her thighs tensed against him, he knew he had his answer. "Are you sure? The beast inside of me is not to be toyed with. Once loose, it's hard to draw back inside."

Mei nodded, a half smile on her beautiful mouth. "Please, *qin ài de*, I want to see."

Instantly, he let his eyes shift, let fangs grow, let claws extend from his fingertips. She only got wetter. Their bodies were hot and slick where they were joined. There was no fear in her when it came to his shifted form. He took his claw and ran it down her slender throat, across the thready pulse that pounded in excitement with the danger. Her jaw dropped, and she tensed. The smell of her pleasure thrilled him, spurring the beast on. Running a sharp claw between her breasts, he circled them slowly, drawing closer to the hard nipples with each dangerous pass. She moaned as if the act only made her all the more desperate in her arousal. Lightly he traced down her sides, letting the sound of his shifted form enter his harsh breathing.

Then, Jarek reached for the sensitive bud

between her thighs. Tweaking it with his sharpened thumb, just enough to make her climax, he grinned. Her body gripped him tightly and cried out in pleasure, still holding his balls. The way she tightened around his massive size was almost painful, but it was a glorious pain. As soon as it was over, she crawled off him.

"But..." Jarek began, glancing down to his still hard member jutting out from his hips. It was covered with her cream, glistening with the evidence of her release. His turgid flesh ached with the need to be released.

"Shh, *qin ài de*," Mei ordered. "Patience. We're just getting started."

MEI WAS a little weak from her climax. It wasn't supposed to have happened so fast, as she'd resisted its pull. But, when the pirate captain touched her clit she couldn't help coming. The man certainly knew how to move. She grinned, very pleased with him. As a lover, he was the perfect choice. She would have to remember to offer the fates special thanks for the gift of him.

Her heart beat heavily in her chest. This wasn't her plan at all. After exploring the ship, she couldn't find the women anywhere. The crew was either sleeping or working and they not once mentioned anything that led her to believe the *pu ren* were onboard. Was it possible they'd left them behind? Mei highly doubted it. Pirates kidnaped and stole. It was their way of life.

Somehow, when she looked down at Jarek, he didn't seem all that bad. His eyes were kind, almost giving. When he touched her, he was passionate yet gentle.

She'd been shocked to see he was naked under the covers. The plan had been to subdue him into telling her where the *pu ren* were. But, as she looked at his sleeping face, all will to fight had drained from her body and she was left feeling nothing but desire. And when he had moved, pulling his covers down, so she saw the tip of his serpent peeking out at her, she had nearly fallen from the ceiling on top of him.

Unfastening the belt at her waist, she stood over him on the bed and let the material slide completely off her body. His eyes narrowed. She saw them easily in the dim light. They were predator's eyes, shifted and golden. His rod was still thick and straight, standing tall in offering. Licking her lips, she knew it had been mean to deny him release, but she wanted to make sure she got her fill. Not only did she need to seduce him to find the *pu ren* and to get back home, she wanted to have these nights of desire before she was forced to marry Prince Lok.

There was freedom in knowing she'd never see Jarek again after they parted. Mei pushed her hair back over her shoulders and gracefully drew her arms down along her body. Her hands glided but didn't caress her own skin, as she gave Jarek's eyes a feast of visual delights.

Mei slowly stroked herself, heating her body anew, purposefully holding back from touching Jarek as he was already in a state of heavy arousal. Her body was a little sore from his deep penetration, but she didn't mind. Out of all her lovers, he was definitely the most endowed.

Her body swayed, and she kicked her foot to the side, turning around so that she stood beside him on the bed, facing away. Jarek moved behind her, and she laughed as his hands eagerly slid along her hips. He kissed her outer thigh, licking a hot trail over her side and butt. Firmly, he turned her around to face him. He licked at her navel, as he touched her everywhere.

Mei stared into his passionate eyes as he looked up at her through the valley of her breasts. When he touched her, his hands were confident, firm, commanding and worshiping at the same time.

Low animalistic sounds came from both of them, as he dipped his head between her thighs.

He took his time touching her, nuzzling his face against her short curls. Light kisses sprinkled along her intimate hairline. His hot mouth closed over her folds, parting them wickedly with his tongue as he kissed her deeply. Jarek lifted her leg up onto his shoulder. Mei gasped. Fingers dug into her hips, holding her to his mouth, as he sucked her clit forcefully. She arched into him, still standing as he knelt before her. Jarek slipped a finger inside her. Cream flooded out of her like never before.

"Jarek," she cried softly. "*Qin ài de!*"

Oh, darling, don't stop, don't stop!

With a very bestial growl, he flipped her onto her back, cradling her body with his arms as he came above her. He kissed her deeply, maneuvering himself between her thighs. He watched her face, taking in every one of her reactions. His long, dark hair fell over her, tickling her. He was gorgeous.

Mei giggled at his forcefulness, feeling giddy and protected by his great strength. She'd never had a lover move her about as if she were as light as a *qizajian*. Slow and sure, Jarek brought his erection to her, and the first probe found her tense and waiting. His eyes burned into hers, and his parted lips hovered just above her mouth. Their breaths mingled until they were taking each other in.

Her body wept cream as he thrust inside her. His shaft stretched her muscles to fit him. With so much control that it drove her mad, he pushed into her slick passage, filling her body by small, agonizing degrees. Her eyes rolled in her head as she waited for the moment he'd stake complete claim to her.

Mei felt as if his essence was filling her, body and soul, as nothing ever had. Their breaths caught at the same moments and released as one. The timing of their union was precise, uncomplicatedly so. Every movement was perfect, joined, as if it was meant to be.

Jarek's sultry dark eyes narrowed as the climax built between them. Each tremble, each tremor was in sync. He pushed back slightly on his hands, but only to look more fully into her eyes as he kept thrusting, slow and deep. The pleasure built until she was mindlessly clawing at his arms, thrusting her body up to him, accepting.

Release hit them explosively. Their bodies tensed, shaking as Jarek emptied himself into her. Mei moaned, the sound echoed by him. A burning need to please him in every way raged within her. In that moment, she wanted to give him everything. The depth of her emotions surprised her. Finally, as the tremors subsided, his lips met hers in a light kiss.

Jarek rolled onto his side, keeping her trapped under his arm. Mei was apprehensive as she refused to look directly at him again. They'd connected somehow. She knew they had. In all her years, she never thought anything like that would ever happen. How could she feel him so deeply? As if his heart beat was hers? As if his soul and hers were merged and inseparable?

I can't trust him. He's a pirate.

Mei took a deep breath, willing her heart to slow. Despite her wanting it not to be so, she was comfortable in his arms. She tried to make herself leave, but she was too relaxed.

Everything happens for a reason.

Her great-grandmother had told her that. Was she on the pirate ship for a reason? Did this journey have something to do with her future?

"What are you thinking about?" Jarek asked.

"Home," Mei answered. It wasn't a lie. She was thinking of home. Now that she'd confirmed he was a shifter, she had to be careful. Many of his kind could sense lies. A shiver racked her as she thought of how his claws and fangs had come out to play. And his voice!

Mmm. Delicious.

He leaned over and kissed her neck, letting his sharper teeth glide over her skin, not hurting her but definitely showing her his power and strength. She liked the primitive, streamlined way his body moved. He was stalking, graceful, and terribly sexy.

She chanced a fleeting look at him. The dark depths of his eyes were streaked heavily with the gold. She liked the shifting of his gaze. The danger of it excited her. It was odd, but she didn't want to lie to him even if she could. Never after sex had she felt so connected to her partner, so fulfilled and spent.

Jarek was everything she'd ever wanted, and he was something she couldn't keep.

16

"Do you miss your home?" Jarek asked softly, as he pulled Mei into his chest. His body was sated, but his mind and soul wanted more of her. It craved her, craved knowing everything about her. There was something about the woman that captured him. And, sacred cats! He didn't mind being lost to her. "Are you sorry you had to run away?"

Mei shrugged, avoiding answering. "Do you have family?"

Jarek wondered why she was refusing to discuss her family. "Mm, yes, four brothers, four sisters married to my brothers, and by now I imagine I have four nephews."

"You don't know for sure?" Mei laughed, but

the sound was a little sad. It was as if she felt sorry for him.

"I..." Jarek sighed. "It's been a while since I've seen them. There were two born, and the other two were carrying when I left home last time, and we've been too far out into space to receive transmissions. But, by my estimation, all of them should have had their sons by now."

"All sons?"

"Yes, we Var can only have sons. Well, almost only. One in a million are born female, so it's unlikely I have any nieces."

"Var," she repeated softly, forming her mouth around the word, trying to mimic his gruffer accent. "Var."

Jarek chuckled as he rolled onto his back and thought of his family. They had been heading home to see them when Rick had been taken. The trip home had to be postponed in order to save him.

"What are their names?" Mei traced a strange pattern over his collarbone and pectoral.

Jarek took a deep breath, nervous to be discussing his family with her. It seemed silly after what they had done together. Part of him wanted her to be impressed. Part of him wanted to hide who he was, wanting to make sure she liked him for being him and not a title of birth. He wasn't Prince Jarek, not here, not in space.

"You don't want to tell me?" Mei sounded hurt. He kissed her temple to reassure her.

"There is Kirill," he began, only to pause. Jarek felt homesick for his family. Kirill was now king of the Var, taking over where their father had ruled. King Attor was killed in battle not long ago. He was a good king, one who worked hard for his people, but he encouraged men to have too much control in the bedroom by drinking *nef*, a drink that calmed the cat-shifters sexually and gave them restraint.

Long ago things had been different for the Var people. It was a wild time, a time when the cat-shifters let emotions rule their heads and their hearts. They acted rashly and purely by instinct. Jarek was inclined to think like his ancestors. Life was too short to hold back from sexual pleasures, from any worldly pleasures. Thankfully, his brothers agreed, and they'd stopped the practice of drinking the stuff.

The old king had been a hard man, who withheld his affection from all of them, including his many wives. Attor had urged the cat-shifters to prove their worth and dependability with emotionless detachment. He taught by example that to prove great prowess in the bedroom showed the promise of prowess in the field of battle, until strength in one meant strength in the other.

Jarek's grandfather had mated with one woman. She had died when Attor was born, and his father had never recovered enough to breed with more women and produce more sons. Although he took women to his bed, he left Attor without any brothers to help lead the Var nation. So, when Attor took over the throne, he became reliant on a few noble houses. One of those house nobles had actually tried to kill his sons, proving that it was wiser to have many children by half mates than risk having a few children by a full life mate.

Quinn was his youngest brother and ambassador for the people. Reid was Commander of the Outlands, and Falke was Commander of the Guards. Officially, Jarek was practicing diplomacy by learning about other cultures. True, it was important for the Var people to know the way of the galaxies, so they were equipped to deal with situations, like when Samantha had kidnaped Falke. But most days, he was just free to do as he wanted when he wanted to do it.

He didn't tell her as much. Instead, he said, "Kirill is the oldest married to Ulyssa. Before she married my brother, she worked as an agent with the Human Intelligence Agency. She was very good at her job."

Kirill, right after his coronation, was the first to fall for a woman. It hadn't surprised them much when he found a life mate. Ulyssa, the new Var queen, was a good woman and made a wonderful match for the cat-shifter leader. She was smart, cunning, and knew how to use a weapon. To her credit, she loved Kirill very much.

"And she gave up her career to be with him?" Mei asked.

"Yes," Jarek answered, not really thinking about it too much. Mei's sweet smell was around him. He liked holding her delicate body to his.

Again, he kept his answers simple. "Tori was a scientist with Exploratory Science Commission. She came to my home planet of Qurilixen to rid it of a biohazardous contaminate. After she had finished, she married my brother Quinn."

Prince Quinn was the Var ambassador. In truth, it wasn't just a biohazardous contaminate that had brought Tori to their planet. She had gone to Qurilixen to rid it of something much worse, bioweaponry. Doctor Tori Elliot was highly intelligent, if not a little overly serious, also a good choice for the royal family.

Jarek's father had brought the bioweaponry to the planet in hopes of killing Lochlann's dragon-shifting kind, the Draig people. Jarek didn't believe in the annihilation of a whole race, no matter how old the quarrel. Luckily, Kirill felt the same way and was working toward peace. The war really was unwarranted, just old prejudices rearing their ugly heads.

"And she gave up her job to be with him?" Mei asked.

"Yes, she did." Jarek glanced down, wondering at the single-mindedness of her questions. "Falke married Samantha after that. We call her Sam."

"And, let me guess, she was something great, and she now gave it up to be with him?"

"Actually, Sam was captain to this very crew, except for Jackson, Loch and myself. She kidnaped my brother and fell in love with him. She decided to stay with him after she brought him home." As an afterthought, he added, "She is very happy with her decision."

Perhaps the biggest shock of all three was when the stoic commander of the cat-shifter armies, Prince Falke, life mated to the space captain who'd abducted him. But Samantha had captured his brother's heart somehow, making the big bad warrior feel. Sam was also highly intelligent, but she was no ex-undercover agent like Ulyssa and no overachiever scientist like Tori. She was, on the other hand, a bit of a hardheaded smartass and the brothers could more than appreciate that quality in her. In fact, to Falke's irritation, they all liked to encourage it. It was payback from when they were younger, and he'd been in charge of their warrior training.

"You know this, but you know not if they have had their babies?" Mei let loose a soft sound of disbelief.

"My sisters were all happy last time I saw them," Jarek defended.

"Ah," was all she said.

Thinking it best to finish his list, he said, "And my twin brother, ah, that means we have the same mother."

"I understand the word."

"His name is Reid. He married a woman who had no place to go and nothing to give up. Her name is Jasmine."

There, he thought, *that should make her happy.*

Jarek had been with Reid when he'd met Jasmine. The woman had been abused and drugged by a man who had forced her into marriage, a marriage that was later proven illegal. Reid had saved her from that and Jasmine in turn had saved Reid from himself. Her illegal first husband was beheaded by the Medical Mafia.

"I wonder if she would see it the same way," Mei grumbled under her breath. Jarek opened his mouth to defend his family further, when she rushed on. "And the boys?"

"My nephews?" Pride welled in him at the thought. Jarek was happy for his brothers' blessings. He liked children, and they seemed to like him. He would be proud to hold his nephews in his arms and to help raise them, as was the cat-shifter way. "What of them?"

"Do any of them have names?" she asked.

"Ah, I only know two." He ran his hand lightly over her arm, pulling her closer as they talked. The words flowed naturally between them.

"And they are?" she prompted, nudging his chest with her head. Jarek picked up a strand of her hair and rubbed its silky texture between his thumb and forefinger.

"For Kirill's son, they picked Korbin. For Quinn's son, they chose Roderic."

Mei was quiet for a while as she lay in his arms.

"They have life mated to them," Jarek said. For some reason he thought he read disapproval in her. "Not half mated."

"I don't understand what that means." She laughed.

"Life mates are when one of my kind marries and is mated to only one woman for the rest of his life. It is a great sacrifice. If a Var's life mate dies, they will be forever alone. Hundreds of years would be a long time to be alone. It is a great sacrifice to be made."

Mei didn't answer. Jarek frowned, wondering why she was bothered by this. It wasn't as if it affected her. His brothers were another story. He worried about what might happen if they ever lost their wives. They would be destroyed.

Life mates were a privilege best reserved for the lower classes—tradesmen, farmers, even hunters and lower ranked soldiers, all men who could ill afford to keep many mates on a planet so barren of women to begin with. His home planet of Qurilixen suffered from blue radiation, which made female children damn near impossible to conceive.

"And let me guess, half mates don't get the courtesy of being the only wife?" Mei asked.

"No, they don't. A Var might take one life mate or many half mates, never both. My father had many wives and all but my twin and I have different mothers."

Okay, why was he sharing so much? It was as if he couldn't stop talking. What had happened? Did he orgasm all his brains out?

"It is a great sacrifice, what my brothers have done."

"You mentioned that," Mei said dryly.

"It isn't wise for us to life mate. Once it is done,

it cannot be undone. We live a long time and pass that long life on to our life mates."

She glanced at him, frowning in confusion.

"We are aided by a mystical power that guides us and our long life is due to the radiation from our blue sun." Jarek paused. He tried to force himself to be quiet, but his mouth wouldn't listen. It was as if a part of him was desperate to tell her everything about himself. Great, now he was like a chatty woman after sex. "But a lot could happen in the hundreds of years a Var lives. If a life mate dies, the widower would be condemned to centuries of heartache. Many have died from such a fate."

Was he repeating himself? It felt like he was repeating himself. He waited for her to speak.

"And what does this family of yours do? Aside from the housewives who bear your brothers' sons?" Mei's tone was low.

Jarek sat up, turning to look her in the eye. There was more to Var women than the way she described it. But, how could he defend what went on in a Var marriage? King Attor wasn't a fine example of it and he'd never been life mated. He'd never even been half mated.

"Well?" she asked.

"They are..." he hesitated, and she lifted a brow. Carefully, he finished, "In politics."

It wasn't a complete lie.

"Ah," she whispered. "Politics. I understand now. They are politician's wives. You are right. For the right person, that can be a full-time job. May they all be blessed with luck in their choices."

Jarek nodded. "Did I ever mention I liked the dinner you cooked? That I was just giving you a hard time when I said I didn't like it?"

He smiled. Mei laughed.

"I knew you liked it!" She jabbed him in the side with her finger. It didn't hurt.

"So, what does your family do?" He'd been monopolizing the conversation with talk of his family. He wanted to know about hers. "All chefs?"

Mei again laughed. It was a sweet sound. "No, I lied. I am no chef."

"Then?"

She smiled secretively and said, "They are also in politics."

Jarek wondered if she was telling the truth. She was too difficult to sense, especially when his libido was in full force. Just feeling her naked body in the bed, so close to him, made it hard to concentrate.

"And you decided to go the other way," she laughed. "I assume that's why you haven't been back. Being a pirate, you aren't good for the family reputation, are you?"

"Something like that," Jarek said.

"So, what, *qin ài de*? You didn't like staying put?

No arranged life mate or half mate waiting for you?"

"Mm, sorry, *fea*, I like moving around. I like adventure." He grinned, glancing down at her breasts. "There was nothing for me there. I wasn't needed."

"Any jealous half mates anywhere that I should know about?" she asked.

"Mm, no, none of those either. Anywhere." His tone dropped, and he couldn't help his wandering gaze as he narrowed in on the thatch of hair between her thighs. "I'm free as a *solar*, whose trilling call echoes over the forests near my childhood home."

"Ah, the pirate captain is a poet."

He shrugged.

"And do you think you'll ever find a woman to tame you?" Mei asked coyly. Just looking at her, he knew she wasn't asking to be that woman. Funny. He had a feeling she was the first woman he'd met who would be up to the task of trying.

"A man does need to have sons," Jarek said quietly.

"Ah, but he does not need to marry for those," Mei said.

"Very true," Jarek answered, though for him it wasn't. To carry his son, a woman would have to be claimed by him. He couldn't bear the idea of taking a baby from its mother, and he wouldn't let the mother take the baby from him. Though, finding a woman willing to sail the high skies was going to be a challenge. Spaceships and alien ports were no place to raise a child, and he wasn't ready to give that life up yet.

"Well, my naughty pirate, what do you say we forget about marriage and life mates and all things serious. They have no place in our bed." Mei turned on her side and reached for his thigh. He was still sitting, and she slid her hand easily up his leg to his rising shaft.

Jarek felt a moment's regret at her easy dismissal of there being more than sex between them, even though he knew she spoke the truth. Pumping her fist over his length, she worked it to a full, pulsing erection. He groaned, tossing back his head in approval.

"Before we go any further, *qin ài de,*" Mei said. "I must have your word on something."

"What's that?"

"I am your woman on this ship, no one else's. I will not be passed around."

Jarek touched her face gently to calm her worry. They had never mistreated a woman in such a way. "Have no fear of that, *fea,* on this ship you are mine. Just mine. And, as long as you are under my protection, no harm will come to you." His voice lowered. "I will protect you, Mei."

I will protect you with my life.

Mei smiled. It was a shy, beautiful smile. Her eyes dipped to his mouth. Jarek watched her in wonder. How was it that she could look so innocent and yet knowing at the same time?

"You have my word of honor on it." He brushed her soft hair back from her face, liking the idea of possessing her in such a way, of being able to declare her as his, even if it was only mistress of his ship. In truth, he couldn't claim her for more even if he'd wanted to. He knew too little about her.

Keep telling yourself that, Jarek.

"Tell me about you, *fea*." He cupped her cheek. "Why were you running?"

"*Shh*," she shook her head in denial. "Later, *qin ài de*. Now I want you to take me again."

It was a command Jarek could not disobey. He pulled Mei into his arms, kissing her deeply. Her mouth was a drug he couldn't get enough of. Her velvety hot tongue slid against his, tangling in a deep, breath-stealing kiss.

Mei pushed him back on the bed, kissing along his throat as she pushed his head roughly back. She ran her hands over his flesh as she licked a wickedly delicious trail down his neck, licking at his nipples, biting lightly down the center of his chest and stomach. Rimming his navel before crawling lower, she finally reached his stiff erection.

Mei kissed along the shaft, working down to the thick base and back up again, before taking the tip into her mouth. Jarek watched as she worked her mouth and hands over him. It was sheer, erotic bliss. When he was close to climaxing, she pulled off and came up over him.

Her hair spilled over her shoulders. It was a glorious sight. She lowered herself onto him, whispering words he could barely understand. Jarek let her have her way, as she set a fast, needy pace. She was a vixen in bed, as insatiable as he was. He couldn't help but stare in wonder as he imagined he'd finally met his match in the bedroom.

Jarek came again with her on top of him, surging everything he had into her warm, trembling body. Afterward, she collapsed against him, their bodies sated. He held her close, not minding the lightness of her weight pressing into him. She fell asleep on his chest, and he let her lay there, as he stayed awake watching over her.

17

Jarek eased Mei off his body, lightly kissing her temple before letting her go. Rolling off the bed so as not to wake her, he swiftly got dressed. He needed to join his crew in repairing the ship. As he left her in his quarters, he took one last, long look. He felt close to Mei on a primal level, but he didn't feel as if he knew her as well as he wished to. He wanted to learn everything about her. It was odd, but not knowing the woman in his bed had never bothered him before. Maybe it was because he needed to trust her to read the map and save Rick. Maybe it was something more, something he didn't want to admit fully to himself quite yet.

Jarek frowned as he walked down the long empty corridor. He took a deep breath before joining his crew. To his surprise, everyone was up and working. They shot him knowing looks.

"Decide to skip your shift, captain?" Lucien teased, even though he didn't stop what he was doing.

"Argh, I told you to wake anyone who didn't show. That included me," he grumbled, giving them a forced smile. Guilt hit him hard. Now was not the time to let distractions in. Rick depended on them. "Someone fill me in. Where are we at?"

"You're doing what you need to do to help Rick," Evan said quietly, so only he could hear. "She's important."

Jarek bit back a weary laugh, wishing not for the first time, that Evan wasn't so astute.

"Communicators are almost finished," Lucien said. "Testing them now. The ship coms should be up and running and good to go. After that, it won't take long before the ship's mainframe is up and running, at least good enough to get us by until… well, until after."

"Excellent," Jarek acknowledged.

"Ugh, there is one thing," Viktor said. "We ended up using a part from the food simulator, so it's permanently broken until we can get to a port that sells spare parts."

The men groaned. Jarek felt like joining them, but refrained.

"Good thing we have Mei," Evan said softly, studying him. Jarek knew he was trying to sense where things were between the captain and his guest. He nodded once at the man and Evan relaxed.

"That's no lie," Dev said.

"She is one stellar cook," Viktor agreed.

"Do you think we can get her to program that stuff into the unit for us before we drop her off wherever she's going?" Lucien asked.

The men turned to him, their expressions hopeful. Jarek chuckled, saying, "I'll see what I can do."

Their sounds of appreciation rang over the engine room. He shook his head. The simulator programming was hardly a high priority, but he understood their desire. It became old eating in space with limited programming.

"We're about done in here," Dev said, bringing the conversation around to business. Jarek studied him. He might be at odds with Rick most of the time, but he was awfully testy about having him missing. Jarek nodded in his direction. They were all worried and worked as fast as they could.

"We should be able to fly out of here in about twelve hours," Lochlann said. "I'll take this ship straight to a space dock station to fuel up, and we'll be on our way back to Lin...tian."

Jarek nodded slowly. He opened his mouth to

answer but stopped when he realized everyone was looking over his shoulder. Turning toward the door, he saw Mei.

She was wearing one of his shirts. The loose black linen was tied at her waist, showing off a narrow strip of skin along her midsection. She'd transformed her gown into a skirt that wrapped her hips with a decorative ruffle down the side from the old neckline and sleeves. If he hadn't seen the robe-like gown before, he would never have known. Jarek licked his lips. His shirt had never looked so good. Black ground shoes covered her feet, and her hair hung over her shoulders in thick dark waves. There was a flushed look to her features, the look a woman got after she'd been in a man's bed. Her eyes were clear, sparkling and unashamed.

Jarek swallowed, at a loss for words. He glanced back to his men. They seemed to suffer from the same thing he did. Their jaws were slack in awe, as they stared at the pretty woman in the doorway.

Dev broke the silence. "Welcome, my lady."

"Thank you," Mei said.

"Ah, *G-gax,*" Lucien stuttered, managing to step forward even as he stumbled over his feet, "*gax-ìng jìan-dào*…um…*n-î*. I am Lucien. I run communications on the ship."

"Pleased to meet you, too, Lucien," Mei answered, taking a step into the engine room. She tilted her head to the side and studied them. Lucien nodded dumbly as if he'd never seen a woman before.

"Oh, hey," Viktor put forth, moving in front of his gawking brother. "I'm Viktor. I'm the ship's mechanic. I can fix anything you need fixed, my lady."

"Pleased to meet you, Viktor," Mei said, a small laugh in her voice. "You are the one who…made me cook?"

"Yeah," Viktor said, his voice airy. Then, as if finally comprehending what she said, he added, "I mean, no, Jarek broke the food simulator. I was going to fix it for you."

Mei lifted a delicate eyebrow.

"But, I can't now," Viktor rushed. "We had to use a part…and… You are really pretty, my lady."

"Mm-hmm," Mei said, thoughtfully. "I do not mind the cooking."

"Ah, Jarek," Lucien sighed, "Can we keep her?"

"Yeah, captain, can we keep her?" Viktor asked, just as breathless. "Please?"

Jarek chuckled. Mei's eyes had narrowed some, but she didn't look concerned. She looked irritated.

"You are the women I saw running?" she whispered, staring at Lucien and Viktor. The crew began laughing, all but the two Dere brothers who looked sheepishly at the ground. Jarek watched, impressed by her quick observation. "You are, aren't you? You are the *pu ren* I saw running away from Emperor Song's palace."

"Ah, well, you see..." Viktor began.

"It's not what you think," Lucien inserted, kicking at the floor. "We didn't like it."

"We don't do that," Viktor added. "You know, wear women's clothing like that."

"We had to," Lucien said.

"You two appeared to enjoy it to me," Lochlann teased wryly. "You begged us to let you keep the gowns."

"We did not," Lucien protested at the same time his brother exclaimed, "No!"

Mei stepped closer, studying all of them intently. Finally, her dark eyes turned to Jarek. His gut tightened in response. She just had that effect on him. He couldn't breathe when she looked directly at him. It was a shock of electricity through his system, as if someone had taken a phazer to his heart.

Sacred cats, she was beautiful! Everything seemed to go into slow motion as he stared at her. His body ached just to be near her. And she intrigued him too. Everything about her utterly and completely fascinated him.

"There are no other women on this ship, are there?" she demanded.

Jarek gave a sheepish grin and shrugged. Stepping forward slowly, she stopped to run her finger lightly over his chest. She looked at him and smiled, completely unashamed by what the others might assume from the gesture. In fact, her eyes claimed him, as did her open expression. Her hand stopped above his heartbeat, and she stood, gazing up at him as if she wanted the crew to know she was his.

"What did you take from Emperor Song?" Mei kept her hand on his chest, as she looked them over, one by one.

Lucien and Viktor cleared their throats and looked away. Evan and Jackson turned back to work on repairs. Dev didn't move. Lochlann grinned.

"Who says we took anything?" Jarek asked, looking down at her. He liked the idea that she wasn't embarrassed to be his woman.

"So, what? You went to Emperor Song's palace just so you could streak through it in women's clothing? And now you're going back there to do it again?" Mei nodded mockingly. "Or is it you are going to look for this Rick who is missing? And, for some reason, you believe Emperor Song has him as a prisoner?"

"We mean no harm to your emperor," Jarek assured her, amazed at her perception.

"Emperor Song?" Mei laughed. "He is not my emperor. Singhai is not my empire."

"You were a prisoner?" Dev asked. Jarek's heart squeezed in his chest to think of her in harm's way. "Have you seen Rick in the prisons? You know him?"

"No. I was a guest of Emperor Song's," Mei said. Her eyes stayed trained on his. "And I don't know your Rick."

"Then why did you try to escape, if you were just a guest?" Jarek didn't really have anything to hide from his crew. Not in this. When it came down to it, regardless of what he was feeling, her presence on the ship affected them all.

Mei lifted a brow and dropped her hand from him. "I wasn't escaping. I was fighting you."

Dev chuckled and held his hand out to Jackson. "You owe me twenty space credits."

Jackson grumbled, but nodded. "Fine."

"You were fighting me?" Jarek smiled.

Mei gasped, pretending to be offended. "As if you couldn't tell."

"You flew into my arms, *fea*," Jarek said, knowing he was being cocky. He couldn't help it. She was too adorable. "I thought you were unable to resist my charm, even from the distance."

"You're such a gentleman." She hit his chest, her tone wry. Walking past him to the engine, she picked up a laser and tapped it in her palm as she studied their repairs. "The least you could do is lie to placate my ego. Pretend I bruised you."

Jarek laughed.

"Your wires are crossed here," Mei said, handing the laser to Lochlann. She turned toward the door. "I'm going to cook something for us to eat. Be in the dining hall in one hour, washed and scrubbed, if you want to dine. I won't wait for you and I will not dine with a group of *lajī yaoguài*."

When she was gone, the men laughed. Jarek stood at the door staring after her.

"What's a *lajī yaoguài?*"

"Blessed stars, if I know," Viktor swore. "But if she doesn't like them, I'm not going to be one."

"Imagine, a little thing like her, bossing us around," Jackson said, chuckling as he shook his head.

"Huh, she's right. We did get the wires crossed." Lochlann studied where Mei had been looking.

"I like her," Lucien announced.

"You like all women," Evan said.

"Ah, true, and they like me." Lucien winked. "But this one is funny. And she attacked the captain, which makes her brave."

"Or very foolish." Evan snipped the wires so Lochlann could fix them.

"I'd say brave," Dev offered, seemingly without emotion.

"How did she know about Rick?" Jarek asked when Mei was no longer in sight.

"Um, yeah, that might have been us. We were talking about him earlier in the hall. She could've been crawling around above us." Lochlann shrugged. "Sorry, didn't think it mattered. Evan said she was all right."

"Evan," Jarek said.

Evan cleared his throat. "Uh, yeah, I might have not been completely forthcoming when we spoke earlier about Lady Mei."

Jarek arched a brow and crossed his arms.

"I might have manipulated the situation just a little." Evan looked guilty.

"Tell me everything. What do you think?" Jarek ordered. "Can we trust her?"

"I don't think we have a choice," Evan said. "She seems comfortable with you, captain. You should show her the map. Her soul is good though there is always a risk that she's hiding something or that her goodness will keep her loyal to others against our purpose."

"I hardly doubt she's in with drug traders if she's good," Dev reasoned.

"I just feel obligated to toss out the warning," Evan said. They all knew he didn't like to be called upon to use his gifts, even though it was sometimes a necessity. He never complained about it, but he did get a melancholy air about him afterward.

"Agreed," Lucien said. "I like her. I think we can trust her."

"You said that already," Viktor scolded. "And I agree too. What harm can there be in it? So what if she knows we have a map."

"Show her," Dev said.

Lochlann and Jackson nodded. Jarek sighed. They were in agreement.

"All right. Let's get this ship up and running. I'll talk to her after we eat." Jarek took a deep breath and motioned Evan to follow him. When they were alone in the corridor, he said dubiously, "Not completely forthcoming? Might have manipulated the situation?"

"I didn't lie, captain, I promise. She is hard to read. But when you appeared she was, ah, very responsive to you as you were to her. I don't think I needed to be telepathic to see that much. The guys see it too."

"Matchmaker is a little out of your area of expertise, isn't it?"

Evan shrugged. "All your brothers seem pretty happy with their mates."

Jarek lifted a brow and crossed his arms over his

chest. "And have I ever indicated I am not happy without one? Have I once said I long for a wife?"

"All right, I'll talk." Evan sighed reluctantly. "When you are around her, I get the same impression I get when your brothers are around their wives. Exactly the same. It's powerful, intense, so strong it makes me shake and a little nauseous. In fact, it's a little hard to be around sometimes, if you must know the truth. To feel that kind of passion and not have it myself is torture. But, to know that Mei is your soul mate and not push you in that direction is unthinkable. I know how stubborn your brothers were about finding wives. Being near Reid and Falke as they stumbled their way around was… well…let's just say I would rather sit in a bath full of Lopen acid leaches. Please, for my sake, captain, don't put me through the hell of having to feel another Var prince find and deny love because of some mistaken, yet understandable, connection to a father who was sufficiently devoid of love and compassion."

Jarek didn't move. Evan took a deep breath and continued.

"I mean, when Falke fell in love with Sam, she wasn't much help in being forthright about her feelings for the commander… But, Reid, he's your twin and, well, that was…" Evan whistled, shaking his head as if he could still feel the stress over

Prince Reid and his wife Jasmine's budding relationship woes. "Whoa. I don't want another one of those on my hands."

Jarek chuckled. "So this is about you?"

"Absolutely. Very much so," Evan agreed, nodding. "Thanks for understanding. Oh, and if you could get in there tonight and fit in a 'marry me' when you're discussing the map that would be great. It would save me weeks of aggravation as you ponder your future desires, only to come to the ultimate conclusion that is so clear to me and very apparent to everyone else, that you and Mei are made for each other, just as your brothers were made for their wives. I'll tell you, captain, you Var men are sure of that from the first moment, even if your minds are reluctant to agree with your innate instincts. I've never seen a race with such a single-minded purpose when it comes to…I don't even know what to call it. A targeting device that hones in on the love object and refuses to set its sights elsewhere until it has it? Yeah, I think that works for an analogy. So, there you have it. Good luck proposing. Don't forget to talk about how you feel when you're with her. You cat-shifters have trouble with that sometimes. And don't forget to ask her to life mate with you. You cat-shifters sometimes forget to ask, just assuming the other party knows about it when it happens. You'll want to say the words out loud and clearly, so she understands what is happening."

Jarek opened his mouth but was speechless.

"Yep, I think that about covers it. Good talk." Evan patted Jarek on the shoulder and, whistling, strode back into the engine room to help the others.

"Great," Jarek grumbled, rubbing his temples. "Just what I need."

18

"Anyway, Rick ended up spending all the scavenger hunt money on renting..." Jackson stopped his tale, suddenly a little red with embarrassment.

Mei giggled and blinked expectantly, looking at him across the table in the dining hall. She was adorable. Jarek grimaced. He knew as soon as the stories started that they were a bad idea. The last thing he wanted was Mei getting the wrong impression of him.

The smell of food wafted over the hall. Lochlann was piloting the craft toward a fueling dock. After looking the system over, they decided that it was safe enough to travel as long as they maintained a constant speed and didn't accelerate. That meant no battles with other ships or they were in trouble. Optimal settings would keep them under hyper speed but above a slow drive through the X quadrant.

Until they docked at the fuel port, there was nothing to do but wait. Mei had cooked another lovely meal of rice, fried vegetables, and seed rolls. Jarek was impressed though he still didn't believe that she was ever a cook by trade. It amazed him how relaxed she was during the meal, as she talked and laughed with his crew. It was as if she'd known them a lifetime.

"Well?" Mei insisted.

"*Uh-hem.   Gal-y…ugh…pl-ate…ah…ma-sion,*" Jackson mumbled, grabbing a bowl of fried rice and lifting it as Mei had showed them how to do. He scooped the food into his mouth. As he chewed, he said with an enthusiastic nod, "Mm, this food is really good. Do you think you can program our simulator with this when we get it fixed?"

"Oh, yeah, great idea," Jarek said. "If you wouldn't mind, that is."

"Mm, yeah," Lucien agreed. He took a big bite and made a show of enjoying it.

"Galaxy Playmates Mansion?" Mei clarified, ignoring the request.

The men choked. Bits of rice flew from Jackson's mouth only to land on Viktor's plate. Viktor stared for a second, shrugged, and took another bite. Lucien shook his head at him.

"A ship full of women. Starts with a *'gal-y'* and ends with *'ma-sion'*. And, from what you've said of Rick, it's not too hard to imagine what you meant." Mei winked.

The men were quiet. They turned to Jarek as if waiting for his cue to react.

Mei laughed. "He sounds interesting. I should like to meet your friend. I really hope you are able to rescue him."

The men relaxed, laughing nervously.

"Galaxy Playmates, eh?" Mei whispered to Jarek at her side. She arched a brow in his direction, seemingly pleased when he looked suitably guilty.

"They're overrated," Jarek said diplomatically, only to clear his throat.

"Very good answer." Mei winked, leaning over to kiss him on the cheek, as if doing so was the most natural thing in the world. "You're so cute when you squirm."

The men laughed heartily.

"You know, you are cute, captain," Jackson teased.

"Adorable," Evan crooned, laughing.

"Very sweet," Lucien said.

"Delightful," Viktor agreed.

Jarek growled, letting the beast enter his voice in warning. His crew didn't look scared. Lucien snorted and threw a small seed covered roll at Jarek. Without blinking, Jarek caught it and popped it in his mouth.

"Mm, delicious," he said as he chewed. Already he was full, but he couldn't seem to stop eating. Then, looking at Mei, his passion for food turned into passion for her. Letting a low rumble enter his words, he whispered to her with meaning, "Very delicious."

Mei blushed, looking down at her plate. She grabbed one of the seed rolls and popped it in her mouth. The men's laughter only grew, and the stories of past voyages started once more.

AFTER DINNER, at Jarek's request, Mei walked with him through the corridors. She easily wrapped her arm around his waist. Her hip brushed his leg as they moved.

Jarek had never felt so relaxed in all his life. It was as if Mei belonged there, at his side, as if she had always been there. He couldn't explain it, and he didn't really want to try. It was what it was. He'd never been so comfortable so fast with any other person.

Evan was right. There was more between them than just a fling. Maybe he'd been wrong with his preconceived notions about relationships. Odd how one night with Mei had changed everything. Though, what Evan hadn't taken into account was that Jarek wasn't like his stubborn brothers. He wasn't one to run from his feelings. It was why he was out in space. His feelings had led him to travel. In a way, it could be concluded that he ran from responsibility into space. Jarek didn't see it that way. He followed his heart.

Jarek wrapped his arm tightly around Mei's back, stopping in the corridor to sweep her into his embrace. The urge to kiss her was strong, and he didn't resist it. Her sweet mouth opened to his, instantly accepting his touch. He groaned as he thoroughly staked claim to her, enjoying the way she moved against him as she wrapped her legs around his waist.

Chuckling, he pulled back, "I've never met anyone like you. Every time I look at you my hands start to sweat. I just have to touch you."

"I know," she teased, kissing him again. She went to deepen it, but he again pulled back. "Is something wrong?"

"I'm serious, Mei," he said. "I've never felt like this with a woman before. I..."

Her eyes saddened somewhat as he said the words and he couldn't finish. She placed a gentle kiss on his cheek and slid her legs off him. He let her down, so she stood before him. Immediately, his body ached to have her close once more.

"I like you, too, Jarek. I've never felt like this either." She sighed, threading her arm through his as he walked her through the corridor. Jarek wondered about her sadness. Maybe she was homesick. Maybe she was worried about her future. Maybe she was too scared to believe him.

And, maybe, there was just something she wasn't telling him. He knew there was plenty he hadn't said to her.

Too fast, a voice whispered in his head. *Too soon.*

MEI STARED at the map Jarek placed before her. They were in his quarters, which made it harder to concentrate. The memories of what they'd done flooded her, stirring up desire when she should be focused on the matter at hand. Her heart beat in heavy thuds against the wall of her chest, and her hands shook. She looked at the parchment for a long time, trying to hold the sudden wash of nausea and fear at bay before glancing up. "Where did you say you found this?"

"In Emperor Song's palace. It's why they were chasing Viktor and Lucien," Jarek answered. "I'm trusting you, Mei. I want to trust you. I...I feel I can trust you."

Mei nodded, swallowing. She believed him. For some reason, when she looked deep into his earnest eyes, she trusted him as well. There were many secrets in Jarek, swimming about in his dark gaze, but when he spoke it was as if all the deceit was gone. Not like before when they were still testing each other, still hiding. The mere physical release they'd shared turned into more, a connection, an opening between them until at times she felt as if his heart beat inside her. Mei was no fool. She knew she had to be careful. Jarek was still a stranger. However, she knew to trust her instincts. The wind had urged her to go after him. Fate had a plan for her in this. It was just a matter of being patient until that plan unraveled.

Waiting for him to continue, she stared at the familiar lines the map depicted, tracing them with her gaze over the new parchment. By her estimation, the map was drawn within the last hundred years, and it was eerily accurate.

"Our friend, Rick, was kidnaped by intergalactic drug traders," he said. "They're pretty ruthless people from what we've discovered. Those types usually are."

"What were you doing dealing with them?" Mei's jaw tightened, and she chewed her bottom lip in thought. Her concentration went from the map to Jarek, though she didn't turn to him. She studied him with all her instincts and training as a negotiator.

"We weren't with them," he answered. Again, she believed him. "Rick, if you haven't guessed, is a bit of a lover boy. He flirted with the wrong woman at the wrong time and got caught up in her game. She was with them, and it is because of her that Rick was kidnaped."

Mei looked up from the map to study his eyes.

"We discovered that they took him to some purple jade mines on your planet. It's why we were at the palace, stealing this map. We needed to find those mines, but it's rumored that the only known map is at Shan Gung Din palace in Singhai. Only, this map is like nothing we've ever seen. We can't read it. Our translators can't translate it. We can't even place which part of Singhai it is. In all honesty, we believe that it may be worthless to us in finding him."

Mei nodded, still staring down. "You are sure they were drug traders?"

"Yes, fairly," Jarek said. "Please, Mei. I swear to you we don't want to hurt anyone or take anything that's not ours. We just want our friend back."

"He may already be dead," Mei said.

Jarek nodded but didn't speak.

"And you may be killed going after him. Not only by the criminals you seek, but also by Song's guards. They don't like outsiders trespassing in their palace or their mines. They barely tolerate them on the planet."

"What else can we do? He's our friend. We have to go after him. Rick would do the same for us."

"You are very honorable, captain," Mei nodded in approval. "And loyal. You do your family justice, even if they don't approve of your choices."

"Mei—"

"This map isn't of the mines," Mei broke in, shivering. If what he said was true, her brother Haun needed to be told. "In truth, you won't find a map leading to the mines anywhere. It is rumored that the way to the mines is hidden within the intricate carving along the walls, floors and ceilings of Shan Gung Din palace. Unless you are shown, you will never find them. The Songs value those mines greatly. They would not let anyone see their location, let alone allow a map to be drawn of it that could be taken out of the palace. You must be taken to the mines. The way is hidden."

"Then this map is worthless," Jarek concluded. He closed his eyes tight.

"Perhaps to you, but not to me. The reason you cannot match the map to the Singhai Empire, is because it is not of the Singhai Empire. It is of Muntong, across the Satlyun River from Singhai."

"Lochlann checked all the landscapes," Jarek

said as if he still clung to the hope that she was wrong, that the map would help them find their friend. "This map doesn't match either side. And when Viktor and Lucien found it, it was under the Singhai symbol."

Mei touched a small river and traced her finger over it, feeling homesick. "I don't know why they had it where they did. But I know the area this map depicts well. I know this river, these landmarks, and buildings. It is of the Honorable City in the Muntong territory."

"Honorable City?"

"It is what we call the Zhang Palace," she answered, thinking of her family. "Emperor Song should not have this. You see these symbols. They tell of the secret chambers within the palace. Only the royal family and a few others should know of them. It means that someone has told the Songs of this. And these markings are the secret passageways beneath the palace." Mei ran her finger along the map. "The treasure room. The crypt beneath the Hall of the Dead, which is beneath the Hall for Worshiping Ancestors."

"How do you know all this, Mei?"

"Because I've seen the rooms. I'm one of the only few people who have," she said. "This map is not of the Lin Yao mines. Not even close."

"Then Rick is lost." Jarek sat back on his bed,

sighing, his face so forlorn that it hurt her physically to see it. She felt sorry for him. He cared deeply for his men, she saw that. Before meeting him, she'd never have thought a pirate would be so caring, so honorable.

"No. I can show you to the Lin Yao mines. I'll take you there myself," Mei said. "Did you make a copy of this map? Is it in your computers?"

"Yes."

"I must insist that you delete them."

"I'll even let you watch me remove it from the system. I have no use for this information. I'm not trying to comprise palace security." Jarek nodded, as he stood looking at her curiously. "If all this is secret, how is it you know what and where everything is?"

"This," Mei said, placing her hand on the map, "is my homeland. And I've seen the mines with my father when I was a young girl."

"That's right. You said your father was a politician," he said softly to himself. "Then you will give us directions and we will go."

"No, I will go with you." She rolled up the map. "And I will present this map to my father."

"I won't have you coming along on a rescue mission." Jarek touched her face. "I want you to stay on the ship where it is safe. I promised to protect you, and that is exactly what I intend to do."

"No, this is my family's home, Jarek." Mei held up the rolled map for emphasis. "Emperor Song should not have had this. And if drug traders are in his mines, I need to see it for myself. I need to know what is there. This affects both dynasties. Innocent people are killed by chandoo, the drugs you suspect are there. We suspect they are there as well. If I can find the proof, millions of my people will be saved."

"Mei, it's not safe. I will tell you what I find. I promise I will never lie to you. I give you my word on that. If drug dealers are there, I'll tell you. I'll record their activities for you, all the information you need to give to your father."

"You will take me with you, Jarek, or I won't tell you where it is. I'm sorry, but that is the way things must be. The Zhang royal family will listen to me, trust me. They don't know you. Your word will mean nothing to them. They will have no reason to trust a pirate. As for the recording, it won't work. The entrance to the mine erases all devices to protect its secret from the outside world."

"Why would the Zhang family listen to you?" Jarek demanded. "If I'm going to let you risk your life and ours by coming along, I must have a better reason. I'll give my information to the royals, and they can make their decision from that. I'll tell them what I saw. If they are responsible, they will act. But first, I will get my man."

"Jarek," Mei took a deep breath. So much had changed with the showing of this map. She suddenly understood why she had been compelled to believe Viktor and Lucien were women, to fight the pirates, to go on Jarek's ship. It was to see this map, to discover that Emperor Song had spies within her family's walls, spies who told him of their secret rooms and passageways. It was to prove that there were drugs in the Lin Yao mines, drugs that hurt the Lintianese people. "They'll take my word because I am a royal."

"What?"

"I'm Princess Zhang Mei. I was in the Shan Gung Din palace to help negotiate with Emperor Song. We sought permission to enter his mines and look for traces of chandoo ourselves. He denied us but promised to look into it. If Emperor Song finds drugs, he will not tell us. There is a possibility he already knows or is involved. We do not trust the Songs. Our dynasties do trade, but we remain separated. That man you saw me with was Prince Zhang Haun, my oldest brother and future emperor to my people. He must know what is happening. So you see, Jarek, I must go with you. It is my duty, and I must see with my own eyes that the drug traders are there. There is no time for anything else." She held up the map. "With this information about our palace, spies will have their eyes on the royal family, and it will be impossible to send guards in without much planning. No one knows why you were there. They won't be expecting you, and they won't be expecting you to come with me. You're a pirate, Jarek. How are they to know you have morals? They will believe that you took me for ransom or to sell."

Jarek didn't move.

"It's what needs to be believed. Otherwise, if you are anything but a common criminal, some might worry that you'll meddle more. We are not scared of thieves, Jarek. We are scared of losing our way of life."

"I promise you, I'm not out to hurt anyone." He touched her cheek briefly and let go.

"And I want to believe that. On some level, I do believe that. But, as a princess, as a royal member of the Zhang family, I am responsible for the welfare of my people. As long as you are what you say you are, there will be no problem. You will ransom me and get away. I'll arrange it with my brother to ensure you escape unharmed, and we'll report that you were destroyed in space, along with the purple jade you were paid with. Quite frankly, you are lucky you found this map. It will ensure my family will be grateful to you. As to kidnapping me, fate acts in mysterious ways. Your friend was kidnaped to take you to the planet, to find this map. You kidnaped me so that I may find this map for my people. Fate. My family will understand that as well when I explain it to them. You and your crew will have my protection."

He didn't move. She could see that he wanted to speak, but he held back.

"If it were your family's lives on the line, all those brothers and nephews and sisters, you would go, wouldn't you? You would go to save them? To protect them? That is how I feel about my people. Similarly with Rick and this crew. Wouldn't you do everything within your power to make sure none of them came to any harm? Aren't you doing just that? I know how scary our borders are to the rest of the galaxy. A lesser person would not risk infiltrating the Song Palace for the life of one crewman. I need to know you understand, that you agree with what I have said."

Jarek nodded once, his lips tight.

"*Xièxie nî,* Jarek. Thank you."

He hesitated and took a deep breath. "Mei, I've lived long enough to know myself and know what I want. I want you. I'm not going to be able to let you go when we get back there. I'll take you to the mines to see what is happening there, and I'll let you tell your family and give them the map, but please Mei, don't make me leave you there when we go."

"Jarek—"

"Mei, I know now what you are. But, I'm asking you, begging you. Choose a different life. Choose the sky." He paused, his voice softening. "Choose me. I swear my life will not dishonor you in any way. I'll make changes if I have to, just don't leave."

Her breath caught and held, as her heart beat a frantic pace in her chest. She hadn't expected that from him. Every part of her wanted to say yes, to yell and scream for joy. Then she looked at the map in her hand—her home, her family, her future.

Princess Song Mei, wife to Song Lok, future Empress Song.

Fate was cruel to tempt her with Jarek's offer.

It was clear to her now that her future was decided because of what would happen after the drugs were found in the mines. She didn't know exactly how things would come about, but in the end it was possible her marriage would save her planet and the Lintianese people. Something as big as spies and intergalactic drug traders in the Lin Yao mines would cause a lot of distrust between the two empires. Now, more than ever, she knew her marriage could be the thing that would save them all from war, from destroying everything they stood for. War would make them weak, would open the empires to the outside world. People would die, possibly even her brothers and childhood friends.

"I can't," she whispered. No two words had ever been so painful to say. "I…can't."

He stiffened, looking as though she'd hit him. Pain rolled through his eyes. "You're right. It's too soon to ask such a thing. It's just…I have strong feelings for you, Mei. I care for you. I don't wish to see you go."

Tears rolled over her cheeks, as she nodded. "This is crazy, I know, but I care for you, too. But we cannot be, Jarek. I have my responsibilities to my country and to my people and family. You cannot know what it is like for a princess. I must put the needs of others above myself."

"Are you married?"

"No," she said, wiping her eyes. "No, I'm not."

"Then, why? Why can't you at least consider it?" Jarek pulled her close. "I'm not asking you to renounce your title, or to forsake your family."

She felt his desire for her pressing tightly against her stomach. It was the same spark that lived within her. A fire burned hot inside her for this man, this pirate captain. "Jarek, I have a family. My brothers, Haun, Jin, Lian, Shen. My sister, Fen. My father and mother. I can't abandon them."

"I know you have duty and honor. I felt it in you the first time I saw you, flying at me from that ship. But the empire can be ruled by others. As you said, you have brothers and sisters and family. They can manage without you if need be. There are plenty of them. Come with me. Stay with me. Let me love you."

"Love me?"

"Yes," he whispered, holding her tighter, "love you."

"Jarek, it is because I have my family there that I must do my duty by them."

"If they need you, I can fly you back. There is no reason why you can't contact them or why they can't find you," he said.

"I will need to contact them immediately," she answered, reminded to do so by his words. "I want to tell them about the mines and this map. My brother won't like me going any more than you do, but I have no choice, and he'll see that."

"As soon as the communications are up. Your brother's ship hit us pretty hard."

"Yes, he's quite proud of the *Ming Tian.*" Her brother's ship was the best on her planet. Haun had put a lot of time and consideration into it.

"Are you not answering my question for a reason? Won't you at least consider staying with me?"

Mei wanted to say yes with all her heart. "I'm sorry, but fate does not see us together."

"How do you know what fate has in store?"

"There is so much we don't know about each other."

"Then tell me. That is why I want you to stay with me. Let us get to know each other and see if the feelings we have are founded. Please, say you'll come with me after we rescue Rick. Just to my homeland. I want you to meet my family. And, after a few months with me, if you hate it then I promise to bring you home."

His family? The idea was tempting. Too tempting.

"Your family?" she whispered.

"I wasn't born a pirate," he said. "My family is noble. Surely that will have some sway with your parents."

"I don't doubt your family's honor, Jarek. But fate—"

"How do you know? Fate brought you to me. You said it yourself."

"I know what fate has in store because it's shown me, Jarek." She couldn't look at him, couldn't bear to see the look in his eyes—so lost, so hurt, so pleading. "I will be married to Song Lok, heir prince to the Song throne."

"Do you love him?" Jarek brushed her hair

from her face before moving to run his hands up and down her back in small circles.

"No, I barely know him." It felt right to be held by Jarek.

"An arranged marriage?"

"Yes, of sorts."

He held her tighter. "What if I don't take you back? I could refuse, run away with you into a distant galaxy."

"Then I'll never forgive you."

"Fine," Jarek sighed heavily but didn't let go. His hands became searching as they dipped along her hips to her butt. He lifted her against him, moaning in the back of his throat as their bodies crushed together. "I'll take you back, Mei, if that is what you truly wish for me to do. I promise."

"I know. You have too much honor in you, as well. I see it in you, Jarek."

"What about us?"

"Lok has nothing to do with us. He may have my hand in marriage, and my people may have my duty and honor, but you shall have my heart Jarek. Please, let's enjoy what we have. I want these memories to last."

Jarek looked away. "You don't know how hard it is to agree with those terms."

"Please, Jarek. For me. This is all I'll ever ask of you. Love me for the time you have me."

"And beyond."

"And you will respect fate? You will let me do what must be done?"

"Only if you ask it."

"I do. I have to. You must understand. The needs of the people must come before the needs of one."

"I understand more than you know."

"I suppose you must. This ship is your kingdom. Just as you go for Rick, you know I must go for my people."

Jarek held her tighter as if he was afraid of letting go. "You do your family a great honor, Mei. I only hope they appreciate you."

"They do. They are good people."

Mei looked up at him. The light was soft, but she could see him clearly. His large body was so protective, his touch so tender and passionate. She ran her hands up over his arms, caressing his strong muscles as she wound her arms around his neck. Her lips parted, silently inviting his kiss. He took the invitation without hesitation.

Mei was sure that's what she liked most about Jarek. He never hesitated when it was something he wanted. When he kissed, it was with total passion. She never wanted him to stop. If he kissed her forever, she would gladly live in the feeling.

Warm hands moved up her sides, moving to rip

the material of the shirt she had borrowed from him. He tore it open, freeing her breasts. She had no underclothing on, and he found her nipples easily. Pressing them with his thumbs, Jarek sent a tremor of pleasure over her body. Her hips jerked and cream pooled in eager acceptance.

"Jarek," she whispered against his mouth. Her worries melted away. She loved looking at his handsome face, but the pleasure of his touch overwhelmed her, and she had to close her eyes.

It was the first time in her life she didn't feel the overpowering press of responsibility lurking in the back of her mind. All her life, she was mindful of what she did, of who would find out, who would see. There was always a sense of paranoia that her actions would be recorded. Lovers had to be carefully selected, the encounters thought out. Few men were worth it, most were chosen out of a physical desire and the need to be close to someone even if it wasn't the perfect someone. But with Jarek, it was different. She didn't fear being seen. The crew looked at her, but they weren't searching for a breach in decorum. She could touch Jarek without guilt, without thought. It was a freedom she relished.

Mei wanted to stay with him, in the stars, out of the spotlight. She wiggled against his body. The silk of her skirt slid between them, gliding their bodies together. His thick arousal settled next to her stomach, pressing into her from beneath his pants. She breathed hard, stirring and rubbing against him. Running her hands along his chest, she pulled at his shirt while trying not to break the contact of his lips.

His mouth was the thing of dreams, passionate and firm, giving and taking. Time blurred within his kiss until all she felt was his flesh pressed to hers. Their clothes were gone, and their bodies moved in a frenzy of caresses. His hands explored her, commanding her flesh as he boldly touched wherever he desired—her breasts, her hips, moving around to cup her firm backside and pulling her forward.

Small sounds of pleasure escaped her, punctuated by the primal, bestial sounds of his groans. With each passing second, his passion became fiercer. He rocked his hips against hers, growling in pleasure as he kissed her. Finally, unable to breathe, she was forced to break the kiss, gasping for air as she tilted her head back.

Jarek lifted her up. He moved in a fiery trail down her throat with his mouth. She felt the dangerous brush of teeth, but everything in her told her to trust him, that he would never hurt her. He nipped her flesh only to soothe the irritation with his long tongue. The harsh sound of their breathing mixed with the pounding of her heart reverberating in her head.

"There is just something about you, Mei," he whispered between heated kisses and playful bites. "I can't stay away."

His hot mouth captured her nipple and he sucked, firmly kissing it before moving to the other side. Mei gasped, flooded with him—his taste, his smell, his touch. A smile curled her lips as he kissed his way lower. His dark head brushed along her stomach, his hair tickling her. He made his way down, his lips brushing between her thighs. Sounds of possession came from him, vibrating against her as he dipped his tongue along her slit.

"Mm," he groaned, kissing harder.

The erotic sight of his face pressed into her was too much. She grabbed his hair. His hands on her hips kept her upright as she climaxed against his mouth. Jarek pulled back with a catlike grin as he sprinkled light kisses up over her body as he stood. With a gentle sweep, he lifted her into his arms. Mei held on tight, panting softly against his neck as he carried her toward where the bed would come out of the wall.

"Computer," he ordered. "Bed."

The bed slid out of the wall, and he laid her on it the second it stopped moving. Mei shivered as they were parted for a brief second. His body came over hers. Without a pause, he slipped his legs between hers. His erection found her wet opening, ready and waiting for him. The taste of her was on his mouth when he kissed her. He groaned, teasing her as he slipped his arousal along her sex. His breath caught, but he did it again, dancing along her opening until she was mad with lust. She stirred against him. The tip of him brushed her clit, stirring her passions until they ignited in tingles over her flesh, setting her thighs aflame.

"*Qin ài de.*" Mei cried out, begging for more. She was wet, more than ready. Her hips lifted, trying to get him to thrust. He grinned, laughing softly in his passion. "Jarek, *mmm*. Please."

He pushed into her slick passage, filling her body by small, agonizing degrees. His eyes bore into hers, taking her in. The light was on, and they could see each other clearly. Mei panted, gasping for air. His hands were on her flesh, dipping between her thighs to heighten her pleasure as he stroked the sensitive bud hidden in her tender folds.

"Jarek," she whispered, over and over, "Jarek, Jarek..."

He finally pressed fully into her, filling her to the brink. Jarek groaned, working his hips in small circles. Mei cried out in mindless pleasure.

"Ah, *fea*, you're so beautiful." Jarek smiled, kissing her.

His eyes stayed on hers. Working his hips, he pumped into her. The pleasure built between them. He didn't look away.

"More," she begged. *"Qin ài de, more!"*

Jarek hit harder and harder with each thrust, lifting up as he moved rapidly within her. She wound her fingers into his long black hair, enjoying the silken length against her palms.

They came at the same time, trembling as wave after wave of intense pleasure shook them to the core. His eyes shifted with golden hues as he filled her with his seed, releasing within her.

"Jarek," she whispered, holding him close.

"I love you, Mei," he said, rolling over so she was on top of him. He wrapped his arms around her and let her lay on his chest. "I want to stay like this forever."

"I've never met anyone like you," she answered.

He chuckled softly. "And you never will again, *fea.*"

20

JAREK HAD NEVER BEEN HAPPIER, but with the sweet came the very bitter, the knowledge that his happiness couldn't last. Because of this, his heart was heavy, and it put a damper on his time with Mei. When he held her, everything seemed right, more right than he'd ever felt in his long life. And, slowly, the realization came that when it was time to leave her on her home planet, he was not going to be able to. The awareness that he would go against her wishes didn't sit well with him. But what else could he do?

He let her believe he was a pirate. One, it seemed to thrill her sexually. Two, she was insistent that if he was anything else, she'd have to take other actions. Besides, he reasoned to himself, he was somewhat of a pirate as well as a prince. It wasn't a lie to let her believe what she wished.

Every day, Mei cooked for the crew, and they ate with relish. It was discovered that Viktor had stockpiled a lot of food in his quarters, just in case she couldn't. The men teased him mercilessly about it, sometimes playfully refusing to let him eat with them as they enjoyed Mei's gourmet dishes. He'd pout, chewing on his hardening Qurilixen blue bread, tormented by the aroma that came from the dining hall. In the end, they always gave in and let him join. It was all in good-natured fun anyway.

When they weren't eating, they were working. Just a few blasts from the Lintianese vessel had caused a lot of damage. By the time the floating space dock was in sight, several days had passed. The ship wasn't a hundred percent, but they couldn't waste any more time.

Mei stood by his side in the cockpit as Lochlann steered the ship through the port doors. The metal of the docking ship looked worn and beaten up. Black scorch marks from laser blasts marred the outside surface. Jarek tensed. This really wasn't the type of place he wanted to bring Mei. He started to worry about what she'd think. If she was used to luxury, would this out-of-the-way space dock convince her that life in space wasn't worth trying.

His jaw tensed as he took in every detail as if

seeing it for the first time. He tried to look at it from a woman's point of view. The dents were glaringly obvious, and the workers looked like they hadn't bathed in days. As *The Conqueror* slipped into place, Lochlann shut down the controls and stood. He stretched his arms as he led the way to the loading dock. Dev was there, already lowering the hatch so they could exit.

"Are you ready?" Jarek whispered. Mei nodded. "I want you to stay by my side."

Mei listened to him and stayed close to his side. Jarek was glad. He didn't want her out of his sight. Glancing down at her, he was surprised to see the wide smile of excitement on her face. Her hand clutched at his arm, but her eyes were all over the dock, taking it in.

One alien, with tentacles drifting like strange arms around his head, locked the ship into place. He made gurgling noises, and every time he touched something, a suction sound popped over the large docking bay. Dev watched him carefully to make sure it was done correctly. The creature didn't seem too happy with the supervision, but one look at Dev kept him from causing a fuss.

"Loch, see to the fuel. Evan, take Lucien and Vik and get supplies and parts." Jarek pulled Mei closer, holding her by the arm with a firm grip. "We're going to see about food."

Evan nodded. Yelling, he called, "Vik, Luc, come on, we need to stock up!"

"Great! We're out of liquor," Lucien answered, sauntering down the plank.

Lochlann waved his hand in the air, motioning a blue humanoid with fuzzy hair over. Evan laughed, and all three trailed off toward an exit. Other creatures were in the docking area as well. Mei lifted her hand in fascination as if to point at a man with blue and silver-scaled flesh that glistened as though he was covered in water. Next to him, an orange man with gills protruding from his face wore a helmet filled with water. He rubbed his webbed hands with a greasy substance that made them shine like the blue man next to him. Jarek grabbed Mei's hand, pulling it back down.

"Don't stare at them. They'll take offense," he ordered quietly. She automatically looked away.

A woman with blue hair and green tinted flesh came from the exit door. She wore a brown fur top that barely covered her two breasts and a swatch of fur and leather around her waist. She was exotically beautiful with large blue eyes that swam like the dancing stars. Her bare feet pointed with each step as if she was about to start dancing. The woman smiled at him, and he nodded politely.

Mei poked him hard in the side. Jarek blinked

in surprise to see her glaring at him. Lightly, he picked her up and placed a kiss on her nose.

"No one compares to you, *fea*," he promised, telling the truth. He was flattered by Mei's jealousy, but it wasn't necessary. He noticed the woman, as he noticed everything around them, but did not look at her with interest.

"Don't you forget it," she said, turning a stern eye to the woman as if she was ready to fight her for rights to 'her man'. The woman tilted her head and continued on her way to a small one- person craft docked in the corner.

"Yeah, you'd better run," Mei mumbled under her breath. Jarek pulled her closer.

The markings along the exit door were universal signs for toilets, decontaminator laser baths, food, and lodging. Jarek would not get accommodations off the ship for the night. Usually, they liked staying off the ship for a change and to get away from each other. Even the closest families needed a break. But, the rooms on the space dock weren't exactly the most luxurious. Some of them were just plain nasty, with space bugs and rodents hiding under every surface.

Jarek walked with Mei toward the exit. "Are you hungry?"

"More like curious," she answered. "This place is fascinating."

"Fascinating?" he mused, looking around. He'd hardly use that word to describe the run- down port.

"Mm, yes. It seems the sort of place to find a *liúmáng...*" Mei tilted her head in concentration. "Ah, *liúmáng,* gangster."

Jarek chuckled, the sound low and throaty. "You're one for danger, aren't you?"

Mei grinned, winking mischievously. "Think you can find some for me?"

Jarek whipped her around, pulling her tightly against him. His erection was thick and hard as it pressed into her softer body. Her deep, rich laugh washed over him, and she wrapped her arms around his neck. He let the beast enter his gaze, and she instantly shivered.

"*Nǐ hǎo měi,*" he whispered.

"You are beautiful as well," she said. "My cat pirate."

"Cat pirate?"

"You know, they have rooms here. We could get one, and you could shift for me like you've been promising to do."

"Mei," he began.

"What? You wouldn't deny me again, would you, *qin ài de?*" She lifted up on her toes, pressing a light, fluttering kiss on his chin. "Don't make me beg. You have no duties on the ship tonight, nothing to repair or see to. The men are taking care of the supplies. I'm sure we can slip away for a few hours."

"You make it hard to resist, princess," he whispered.

"Then don't." She kissed him again, unashamed, bold. Her mouth opened to claim his, her tongue wrestling its way past his teeth. A throat cleared, but they ignored it. They were standing in the way, but he didn't care. Jarek felt someone rudely pushing past him to get through the exit. He was thrust forward until Mei's back was flush against the door frame.

"Captain!"

Jarek barely heard the word.

"Captain Jarek!" It was Dev.

Gulping for air, he pulled back. Mei's eyes were glazed with passion, and her smell was all around him.

Jarek couldn't speak, as he turned to acknowledge his friend.

"This guy says they have someone here who can help with repairs," Dev spoke loudly, not moving any closer to them as he stood by the ship. "We're in luck, it's an engineer from Letame."

Jarek nodded. Letames were famous for their telepathic-like abilities. Except, they didn't read each other minds, or even other creatures, they read and controlled metal and electricity. The Letames were rare. Most of their race had been wiped out by greed, and there were rumors that some had been experimented on by the Medical Mafia, who sought to harness their gifts. For a Letame to even admit to his heritage was an amazing thing.

"Fine," Jarek yelled.

"He'll need everyone else off the ship," Dev called.

Jarek lifted his hand and nodded. It looked as if they'd be getting rooms on the space dock after all.

"I'll stand guard tonight," Dev added. Jarek nodded, but the man was already climbing up the loading plank.

"The map of the Honorable City," Mei whispered in concern.

"We'll get it. Don't worry." Jarek turned and headed back to the ship for the map. Mei was by his side.

21

THE ROOM JAREK was able to buy for the night was worse than he could've imagined. It was a small square, no bigger than a class five prison hold in the poorest of districts. The lights flickered and buzzed, annoyingly so. Black grates covered the walls, complete with hooks for hanging clothing. There was no private decontaminator, only the public one accessed from the corridor near the diner.

The walls were punctured with holes. Thick material had been stuffed in them for privacy, held in place by the grates. On one side of them, behind the wall, odd music played, eerie and low vocals backed by some sort of string instrument.

Jarek took a deep breath, embarrassed that he had Mei in such a place. Sacred cats! How was he going to convince her that life with him was where she belonged? Sure, she seemed enthralled now, but this was a trip, an adventure. As a lifestyle choice, it wouldn't be so glamorous. Any hope he harbored of convincing her to choose him faded. He'd have to force her to stay with him.

I'll think about that later.

Sitting on the woven mat on the floor, he put the map of the Honorable City behind him and looked up at Mei. She walked around the room, lightly touching everything within her reach.

"I don't think I've ever been anywhere so dirty," Mei said. As the words left her, a ten-legged bug crawled over the floor. Three eyes spun around in the creature's dark brown head. It was the size of Mei's foot. She yelped, jumping over it to be next to Jarek. "Can we go back to the ship? I think I've changed my mind."

"Ah, come here, *fea*. Perhaps I can make you forget where you are." Jarek lifted his hand to her.

Mei took it but pulled instead of joining him on the mat. "You, my pirate, are going to take me to dine."

"Am I?"

"Mm, yes, you most certainly are."

"*Hâo ba*," he said reluctantly. "If I have to."

Mei giggled. "Yes, *fea*, you have to."

Jarek grimaced. "Men are not *feas*."

"Really?" she said coyly. "What is a *fea* anyway?"

"Long ago, before my people settled on our planet, it is rumored that there were beautiful women, tinier than my thumb. They flew about on gossamer wings and sprinkled magical dust over Var men, making them crazy with love, until they would do anything the little *feas* asked. They were enslaved by love."

Mei smiled. "Is that how you see me, Jarek? As your little *fea*?"

"It's exactly as I see you. You are my *fea*. The first moment I saw you I fell under your spell."

Mei laughed, tossing back her head. "Those were my feet I hit you with, *qin ài de*."

"I remember it as magic."

"You're delusional."

"It's possible."

"Come on, pirate," Mei pulled on his shirt collar. "Buy me dinner."

Jarek laughed, following her. "Whatever you say, princess."

THE DINER WAS small and old, but at least it was clean. Mei took in everything. It was the first time she'd ever been just an ordinary person in public. No one knew of her title. No one bowed or paid her more than a passing notice. Well, that wasn't completely true. A few of the humanoid males paid her notice and Jarek, like a truly possessive man, growled and threatened them with his cat eyes and fangs. He even lifted a clawed finger to one of them who dared to step too close to their table.

Mei found she didn't mind his possessiveness. She liked being protected by him though she was sure she could take care of herself if it came down to a fight. A short, round gelatinous woman brought them plates of food and dropped them on the table with a clank. They hadn't even ordered.

"Psychic?" Mei asked her.

"Only thing we got," the woman answered, her tone husky. Her dress hugged tightly to her frame. It was pink with little red flowers, an odd contrast to her green skin and blue hair though both were darker than the woman who'd flirted with Jarek on the docks. The woman waddled away.

"You know how to treat a girl," Mei teased. Jarek's face fell slightly, and he glanced around. Reaching out, she touched his hand, drawing his attention back. "Hey, I was only joking."

"What? Oh, I know, *fea*." Jarek took up a skewer and stabbed a chuck of meat on his chipped plate. Biting it off, he chewed thoughtfully. "It's not bad."

He sounded unconvincing. Mei was a little more delicate as she poked at a piece of meat. Slowly, she brought it to her mouth, touching it with the tip of her tongue. The sauce was tangy and sweet, with an odd flavoring she couldn't place. It wasn't exactly appetizing. Finding her bravery, she popped the whole piece in her mouth. She did her best not to taste it as she swallowed the meat whole.

Mei was well aware of Jarek's eyes on her and did her best to smile and pretend that she enjoyed it. He was unusually silent as they dined. She tried a few times to start a conversation, but in the end contented herself with observing her surroundings. There wasn't much to see. A hairy, smelly beast of a man sat with another pale man with red eyes. At least Mei thought they were both men. It was a little difficult to tell.

"Hey, captain," Evan said, sliding into the seat next to Jarek. He leaned over and picked up a piece of meat with his fingers and popped it into his mouth. "Ship's all stocked."

"Well, almost all," Viktor said, sitting next to Mei. He motioned to her plate. "You done with this?"

Mei laughed quietly and slid it over to him.

Viktor took a bite. "Mm, just like the prison guards used to make."

"Ah, food, great," Lucien pushed his brother over, squishing Mei next to the wall. He took a bite off Viktor's plate.

"Hey, get your own," Viktor protested.

"Hey, cap. We're in luck. Most of their available supplies consist of liquor." Lucien ignored his brother, continuing to eat off the plate.

"How is that lucky?" Mei asked.

Lucien looked confused. Dumbfounded, he said, "Liquor."

Jarek shook his head. "Talk like that and we'll begin thinking you have a problem. Dev will put you in quarantine again."

Mei looked at Jarek. He smiled at his men, laughed even, but there was something in his eyes when he looked at her—a sadness and regret.

"Yeah, but that wasn't for liquor," Lucien said. "That was because I let a couple of prostitutes into his room."

"Is Dev celibate?" Mei asked in surprise. Sure, the man was stoic, but she never thought of him as lacking in female attention. There had to be some women who found big, red men attractive.

"What? No," Jarek said. "Just particular."

Lucien's face fell. Under his breath, he said, "I didn't know they'd scare that easily. I thought I was doing the guy a favor. He's always so grumpy."

"Ho, Dev!" Viktor called, shutting his brother up.

"There was not much wrong with the ship. The Letame has it fixed. We can take off as soon as they finish loading the fuel." Dev said, joining them at the table. Looking down at the plates, he took a deep sniff. "Mm, Elteeb Stew."

"Elteeb?" Mei asked, looking down.

"Yes, I would recognize the smell anywhere." Dev nodded, ever stern.

"What exactly is an Elteeb?" she asked, wondering how she could've been so preoccupied with Jarek that she hadn't thought to ask what it was they were being served.

"They are a brown, small insect with six to twelve legs depending on their age." Dev held out his hands several inches apart. "About this big."

"Three eyes?" Mei asked, staring at the now empty plate. Her stomach lurched. The bug in their room?

"Yes," Dev nodded.

"*Qù tamade*!" Mei gasped, surging to her feet. She managed to clear the table with her knees as she hopped onto the bench seat. Jumping, she held her hand over her mouth and used the tabletop to step on as she passed through the men toward the door.

"Mei," she heard Jarek say behind her. "Come on, guys, move. Mei, wait."

Mei didn't stop. She ran into the hall. The image of the bug scurrying across the floor wouldn't leave her mind. Gagging, she couldn't hold it back any longer. She threw up on the corridor floor. Jarek was behind her in an instant, holding her up. An old cleaning droid came out of the wall. It moved slowly, but it began to clean the mess.

Mei held her stomach and closed her eyes. For a long time, she stayed bent over, unmoving as she took slow breaths. When she could finally speak, she said, "I ate bugs."

"Zhè bìng bù huài," Jarek soothed. "It's not that bad."

She gave a disheartened laugh. "I want to go back."

"We'll leave shortly for Lintian," he said, his tone hard.

She glanced back at him. A light sheen of sweat covered her flesh, making her feel clammy. Trying not to think of the bug stew, she studied him carefully. Was the sweetheart period suddenly over? Had he grown tired of her already? She'd meant back to the ship, not the planet though that is where she would ultimately end up.

"Good," she answered, not saying what was in her heart. What had happened? Before, what they felt, they just said. Now she was compelled to hold back. Was it because they were halfway through their journey? Was this a silent understanding that distance would make the split easiest for both of them? If it was supposed to be, Mei didn't understand it. Nothing would make leaving him easier.

"Let's board." Jarek led her by the arm, half supporting her weight as she leaned into him. "You look like you could use some rest."

"We have to go and get the map first," Mei said. "We left it in the room."

Jarek frowned but nodded once. They walked in silence. Jarek opened the room door and disappeared. Mei thought briefly of the romantic evening she'd envisioned. There was no way she'd be getting romantic in bug-infested quarters.

"Did you move it?" Jarek asked.

Mei shook to her senses, pulling her gaze from the floor where she'd been searching for insects. "No. It was on the bed."

Jarek turned, his eyes completely shifted. His nostrils flared. "Someone's been here."

Mei ran to the door and looked down the corridor. She tried to listen to the wind, but the air in the corridor didn't stir. That was the trouble with being in outer space. No wind.

Her heartbeat kicked into high gear, and her body tensed. Jarek moved behind her. She turned, just in time to see his body shifting into that of a large cat. Black stripes streaked across his orange back. The fur on his face was white and black. He stared at her from the hot depths of his eyes and let loose a low grumble in the back of his throat.

Mei had teased him about shifting, but in her head it wasn't completely real until that moment. He growled louder, lifting his big head. She saw his fangs as he opened his mouth. The sharp teeth frightened her. Stumbling out of his way, her back hit the metal grate along the wall. A hook poked into her shoulder, and she was unable to slide away from him. Rumors that some shifters couldn't control themselves in shifted form entered her mind. Was Jarek one of those? Was that why he never showed her this side of him? She'd asked on the ship, but he always had something else to do—repairs, flying, making love to her. Mei hadn't pressed the issue.

"J..." She tried to speak his name. Only a whisper made it past her lips. She closed her mouth and stayed completely still.

Jarek's cat eyes narrowed. They were the familiar dark brown and green she'd seen before, the pupils oblong. Deadly claws poked from his thick paws. There was no doubt he was built for killing.

A loud roar escaped his lips. Mei shrieked in fright, forgetting all her training as he leaped toward the door. She shut her eyes tightly. The sound of claws clicking against metal jolted them back open. With a gasp, she looked down. Jarek was gone. He'd gone out of the door. Suddenly, she realized he'd been trying to get her out of his way so he could find the map.

Taking off after him, she caught sight of his tail as he turned a corner. Mei ran faster. He was going toward the dining car.

Jarek's four powerful legs pushed off the floor, showing his graceful elegance and strength of movement. He leaped into the air, flying out of her eyesight as he went through the diner doorway.

Mei skidded to a stop at the diner's door. Jarek's crew was gone, all but Dev, who had a full helping of Elteeb Stew.

The hairy beast with the foul smell jumped from his seat at her entrance. Scraggly brown fur tufts sprouted from his body, knotting into an accumulation of matted fur. Bright green filled his eyes, blocking out the rounded orbs.

Dev fisted his hands, facing the two humanoid men. There were many species in the galaxies, too many to memorize unless you dedicated your life to doing so. Mei was surprised at how tall the hairy beast was at full height. He even towered over Dev and was just as broad.

Mei tensed as Jarek squared off with the beast man. Suddenly, they both lunged. A flurry of movement overtook the diner at once. The gelatinous waitress disappeared through a round side door. The beast's pale friend's eyes glowed with an eerie red. He stood back, out of the way of the flying claws and biting fangs.

Mei watched the fight, waiting for a chance to help and knowing that, like the men on her planet, he wouldn't appreciate her jumping in. Tension practically snapped through the room. Jarek roared. The beast growled. They both drew blood from the other. The beast slashed Jarek's shoulder. Jarek retaliated by sinking his teeth into his hairy arm.

Movement by the round door caught Mei's attention. The pale man was making an escape. Dev saw it too. He made a move to lunge past the fighting men. The beast man slashed at Dev, viciously hitting his chest and slicing it open. Mei took her chance. She ran behind Jarek. A light stirring of the air fanned her cheek, accompanied by a whistling. The beast had swiped at her.

She didn't stop as she darted through the round door, leaning under its frame. The corridor was worse than the rest of the space dock. Dim light made it difficult to see. It shone from a narrow strip along the wall, leading down the passage horizontally like a rail. A few of the Elteebs scurried along the corridor floor, disappearing and reappearing from holes in the wall. Some even clung to the ceilings. Mei shivered, forcing herself to make her way forward. She refused to think that this was where her meal had come from.

The further she walked, the worse the corridor smelled. Picking up her pace, she steeled herself for a fight. She couldn't let the pale man escape, not if he had the map. A slash of light fluttered across the hall, and she detected the unmistakable odor of perfume.

"Where are you?" she muttered, narrowing her eyes. "*Chùsheng xai-jiao de xiang huo.*"

"Such violent words for such a little girl."

The words were a whisper along her ear. She jolted, turning around, hands lifted in readiness. Nothing was there.

"Mm, good form," he said, the voice still soft. "Nice. Firm."

"I was well *trained*," Mei rotated, kicking out with her heel. The last word was strained as she tried to strike him. Her foot hit air.

"I wasn't talking about your fighting skills," the voice mocked.

Mei felt a hand brush past her butt, squeezing lightly. She struck instantly, refusing to let him distract her. This time she hit him. Her fist hit his jaw, sending him sprawling backward. His white skin practically glowed in the dim lights as the pale man got to his feet. He rubbed his jaw, and his red eyes widened.

"You hit me," he accused.

"Um, yeah, that was the point of trying to punch you," Mei answered with a smirk.

He adjusted his jaw. "You will pay for that, little girl."

Mei took his challenge, not thinking beyond the moment. She struck out with her fists, using a combination of punches. Several of them landed.

The man punched, his fist cracking across her jaw. Mei winced but didn't stop. It wasn't the first time she'd been hit, but it was definitely one of the harder blows.

Angry, she fought vigorously. A blind instinct overcame her until she didn't even plan what she was doing. Suddenly, she flipped the pale man over her shoulder, and he slammed onto the floor, dazed. Breathing hard, she stood over him, hands raised. Haun had practiced endlessly with his little sisters until they could throw men three times their size.

"And you just got your ass kicked by a little girl," she hissed. The man groaned, his eyelids heavy as he lightly rocked his head back and forth.

Without wasting time, she knelt beside him and began searching him for the map. Running her hand up and down his thighs, only to work her way up to his hips.

"Mei? Mei!"

Mei glanced up at Jarek's yell. To her surprise, the naked pirate captain was shifted back to his human form. Blood trickled from wounds on his body, several on his shoulders, one on his cheek and a couple on his legs. His long dark hair flew behind him, rippling as he came near. Mei lost her breath as she looked at him. Swallowing, she made a move to continue her search.

"Mei, what are you doing?" he demanded.

"I'm finding…" She never got the words out. The pale man's eyes met hers and he swung. His hand met her cheek, knocking her into the wall. A loud pop sounded in her head, and her eyesight dimmed.

She heard Jarek roaring, but he sounded far away. As darkness overtook her senses, the sound of his voice faded.

"Mei? Me…"

JAREK CURSED as Mei slumped to the side of the corridor. The pale man she'd been searching was on his feet and a blur of movement before Jarek could even reach them. He was one of the fastest creatures Jarek had ever seen.

Though he wanted to pursue, he knew Mei needed him more. Skidding to a stop by her side, he quickly checked her for injuries before sweeping her up into his arms. He stalked toward the diner, holding Mei close.

Tension knotted his shoulders, working its way down to his tight stomach. Worry held him in its grip. He was supposed to protect Mei. He'd *promised* to protect her. And he had failed.

Ducking under the door, he didn't stop as he

stepped over the unconscious lykan and made his way to the ship. Mei's arm flopped in front of him as he walked. Jarek readjusted her body as he made his way up the docking plank.

"Get us out of here," he commanded Evan as the man hit the switch to raise the plank.

"On it," Evan answered, running toward the cockpit.

Jarek swore. He took Mei straight to the medical booth. The ship jerked as the engines kicked on.

"Sacred Cats, Mei. Why didn't you stay where I could protect you?"

23

Mei groaned holding her head. Blinking, she looked around. She was in Jarek's quarters on the ship. It took a moment, but suddenly the flood of memories invaded her mind and she sat up, gasping, "Map."

"Shh, we got it," Jarek said, urging her back down on the bed. He touched her forehead, stroking back her hair to comfort her.

Mei looked up at him in question. "The pale man?"

"Escaped."

"I mean did he have the map?"

"No, the lykan did." At the words Jarek's expression hardened somewhat.

"What is it?" Mei tried to sit up again, but his hands held her back. "Oh, my…Dev? Is he…"

"Dev is fine. You're the only one who was hurt." Suddenly, his expression changed, becoming both tortured and angered at the same time. "Sacred cats, Mei! Do you realize you could've been killed? What were you doing running after someone like that? What if he'd had friends with him? What if he… What if he killed you? Did you even stop to think?"

"I'm sorry, Jarek, I…" Mei frowned. "Wait, why am I apologizing to you? I can take care of myself. What if Mr. Pale Face had the map? While you were busy fighting the giant hairball, he would've got away with it. I did what I had to do to protect my family."

"He didn't have the map. You should have trusted me to handle it." His hand stilled on her head.

"He could have had it." Mei swatted his hand away as she moved to a sitting position. Jarek tried to touch her again, and she slapped him. Inching her way to the end of the bed, she stood.

"No, the lykan had it. It was the lykan's scent I detected in my room, and if you know anything about the race, you would know they are secretive, greedy and not prone to sharing, even with friends." Jarek's lips pressed into a harsh line, and he glared at her. It was almost as if he was scared of moving.

"How was I to know that?" Mei sighed. Why was he being like this? Why was he looking at her so coldly? So angrily? Lifting her chin, she kept her face stoic. "We should take off. We don't want any more trouble. The sooner we are off this planet the better."

"We're almost to Lintian." He lowered his eyes.

Mei gasped, shocked. She looked around as if she could see through the metal walls. Already? How long had she been knocked out? Desperation overwhelmed her.

"We are?" She wasn't ready to leave him. What had happened to her time with him? It couldn't be over already. Studying his tough expression, she couldn't help but wonder if he still loved her. Were his feelings for her only a crush to begin with? A way to pass the time? The way her heart ached, she knew that when she said she loved him, she'd spoken the truth. "Jarek, I want to speak with you. About us..."

"Mei," he hesitated. Passion swirled in his eyes, melting the cold anger. It looked like there was so much he wanted to say, and yet he wasn't saying any of it. Instead, his tone even, he said, "We are orbiting on the side of the Singhai Empire. Lochlann is awaiting your directions on where to land."

"I should contact my family." She glanced down to the big shirt she wore. It was one of his.

"I apologize, *fea*, but the communicators are out. You can't contact your family yet." As he spoke, he stood, crossing over to a metal cabinet embedded into the wall. Running his hands over the sensors, he opened the drawer and took out some folded clothing. "Viktor and Lucien are working on it, but it doesn't look good. I'm sorry that I can't drop you off there before we get Rick, but I can't risk anyone knowing we're here until we discern what's happened to our friend."

Mei shook her head. Closing her eyes briefly, she swallowed back her pain and focused on what needed to be done. It was becoming clear that Jarek wasn't too comfortable with saying good bye. Maybe that was why he was acting the way he was. "That's all right. Perhaps it would be best if I don't contact my family until we've been to the mines, and I know more."

Mei's father and brother wouldn't want her going to the mines without them, if at all, just as Jarek didn't want her to. They would order her home. She understood their worry, but she had to see her plan through. Besides, the sooner she called them, the sooner she'd never see Jarek again. It might be foolish, but she wanted to cling to every moment. Already she was upset at missing the trip from the space port to her home planet. She must have been unconscious a long time.

"I'm going to miss you, *qin ài de*," she said softly. "I need you to know that. I need you to know that this isn't just some space fling that I'll get over quickly. I need to know that you'll remember me fondly, but also that you'll go on to find happiness. I need to know that you'll be happy."

"Mei, I'm..." He stopped, taking a deep breath, only to let a soft curse leave his lips as he exhaled. "I'm sorry I was angry with you, *fea*." Instantly coming forward, he pulled her tightly into his arms. He held her close, running his hand over her head, patting down her hair as he continued. "I was just so scared that I wasn't able to protect you."

"Jarek," she whispered. A tear slipped over her cheek. "I don't want our time together to be over."

"It doesn't have to end, Mei," he said. "You can still come with me."

"I have to marry Prince Lok," she said. "It's my duty."

"But you told me you are not engaged to him. Together we can change that fate. We can carve our own destiny."

"My family—"

"If you fear your family won't accept me, then they will accept my title." He took a deep breath.

His eyes pleaded with her to stay with him, to trust him, to love him.

"What do you mean title?"

He tensed. "Mei, there's something I haven't told you. I am Prince Jarek of the Var by birth."

"You…are a prince?" she asked, surprised. Mei looked over his pirate attire. "Royalty? You? A pirate?"

"Yes. No. A prince, yes, a pirate, not really."

"You lied to me?" Mei was too weak to move. His hands gripped her arms, not painful, but definitely not letting go.

"No, not a lie. You assumed I was a pirate and I…" He pulled her closer. His face lowered toward hers as he looked deep into her eyes. "Here, in space, I'm Captain Jarek, leader of this crew. I never use the title unless I have to, like when I have to represent my family as an ambassador. Let your family have the title to satisfy them. My family will accept you into their arms willingly with or without yours."

"But…" She frowned, confused. "Are you exiled? You do not rule from your palace?"

"I might not live in the palace, but my duty never diminishes. If their future depended on my sacrificing myself, I would. I know I would. But the truth is, I'm not needed." He laughed quietly, lowering his mouth, so it was close to hers. "They have everything well in hand, and my knowledge of space and other cultures comes in handy when my family must leave our planet."

She wanted to pull him closer until their mouths were pressed together in heated kisses, until their bodies melted and became one, but she was too shocked by his revelation to move. Jarek? A prince? She could easily understand his position, maybe better than most because she was what he was. Royalty. There was a burden on them, a self-lessness they must bear. But, even for all his freedom, she could still feel the burden of his upbringing.

"See, Mei, you can still be loyal to your family and not live within the palace. I can still be of service by being in the stars. If my family needs me, all they have to do is call. It works. At first they were upset about my decision, but now they accept it. They have even come to depend upon it. The knowledge I have of the galaxy could not be gained by staying on Qurilixen. Let me show you the freedom of the skies and we'll visit our homelands whenever we wish."

Mei understood this. He might not be running away from his princely duties, but he wasn't running toward them either. However, unlike Jarek's family, her family did need her back on her planet. For that reason, she envied him.

"Why couldn't you have crossed my path first? Why couldn't you have kidnaped me before I went to Prince Lok's palace? Why did I have to talk to him first?" Mei knew the answers. Prince Lok and her marriage would assure peace.

"I don't understand."

"I just wish fate could have been different." Mei dropped her head against his chest. Her head ached, and her neck was sore. Jarek's hands instantly went to her shoulder and began to rub up her neck, as if he could sense her discomfort. Mei moaned. His hands felt so nice, so comforting as they dipped up and down along her spine. "We should land at nightfall."

"We will."

"How much time does that leave us?"

"A few hours."

"Mm, too long a time to wait and think about what must happen, and too short of a time until we have to part." Mei sighed. "Will you make love to me again?"

Jarek answered with a kiss. His touch was soft and tender as he held her close. There was so much passion in his embrace, but also a sadness she could feel as well as her own. They knew this moment would come, yet they weren't ready for it. Fate was a cruel mistress to give her this man only to take him away. Her pirate prince. Her Jarek.

"*Wo ai ni,*" she whispered.

Jarek pulled away just enough to gaze into her eyes. "And I love you, *fea.*"

What else could really be said between them that hadn't been already said? His dark gaze flecked with gold. How perfect those eyes were to her. How handsome this man was. Her heart broke at the idea of leaving him, and she knew that it would never beat in such a way for any other.

"Jarek, will you make me a half mate?" she asked. "I can't marry you, but..."

He gave her a sheepish grin. "That happened the first time we were together when I came inside you and our spirits joined."

Mei rounded her eyes. "Are there any other secrets you want to confess, prince?"

He kissed her as soon as the words left her mouth. His tongue rimmed the edge of her lips. It was a sweet distraction. Between ever deepening kisses, he said, "None...that...I want...to talk... about...right now, *fea.*"

Mei giggled as he prevented her from answering. Jarek swept her up into his arms and laid her on the bed. His greater weight held her down as he pulled at the shirt she wore, parting the soft linen so he could devour her neck and chest with hot, wet kisses.

Sitting back on the bed, he pulled off his shirt.

Jarek always looked so sexy, no matter what he was doing. The light contrasted the tight muscles of his chest and flat stomach. He brought his half-naked body next to hers once more. Digging his hands beneath the shirt, he found the warm flesh of her sides beneath it. A light sound left her, prompting him to resume licking and nibbling at her neck.

"*Nǐ hǎo měi.*" Mei said, squirming beneath his touch. It felt so good. She worked her legs restlessly against his thighs, hooking around him as she naturally angled her body toward his. "You are so beautiful."

Jarek chuckled. "You are the beautiful one, *fea*. I could look at you forever."

His eyes roamed down over her body. They stopped at her breasts. Leaning over, he massaged a small globe in his palm, circling the nipple with his thumb until it was a hard bud.

She lazily returned his kiss, sucking his long tongue into her mouth. Little whimpers left her throat, begging him to continue. Running her hands over the firm muscles of his arms, she caressed him everywhere she could reach. They'd made love often, and she had his body memorized. It was a memory she'd keep with her in the long years ahead.

Grandmother, please be wrong. Please be wrong. Please be wrong.

The thought repeated in her head like a desperate prayer.

Please be wrong. I don't think I can leave him.

And yet she knew in her heart that she couldn't risk the welfare of her people. Self-sacrifice was part of her life. How could she be happy with Jarek knowing she would possibly sign the death warrant of so many by not marrying Lok after the drug trade became known?

As her leg worked up against his stiff erection, he glided his hands boldly down over her flat stomach to dip between her thighs. Her body was wet and ready for him. Jarek growled low in the back of his throat. The sound made her shiver with desire, and she remembered the dangerous side of him as he'd shifted into a tiger. He always had that effect on her. Just one look, and she was wet and ready for him. The fact that he liked sex with her as much as she did with him was exhilarating. She pressed her fingers lightly against his shoulders, and he grinned against her mouth, knowing what she wanted.

He worshiped her with his lips, kissing between her breasts only to drag his tongue over her stomach. Rimming her navel, he reached for her hips, jerking her silk skirt up to expose her thighs. Her legs parted in natural invitation. His long hair tickled her flesh as he explored her with his mouth.

He adjusted her knees over his shoulders and his hot mouth latched onto her awaiting clit.

Jarek moved his tongue, pressing it along her sensitive folds, parting her, drinking in her taste. He sighed in pleasure. She moaned loudly, thrusting her hands into his hair to guide his movements.

"*Bâobèi*," she gasped. "My love, don't stop."

He became more aggressive. Mei tensed on the precipice of intense pleasure. His tongue stroked just right. She screamed, clamping down on his head with her thighs. He grinned and instantly shot up along her body to cover her mouth with his.

"Mm, Jarek. Sweet Jarek." Her hips bucked, rubbing her moist folds along his hard stomach, wanting more of him, wanting it all.

Jarek rose up to unlace his pants. Once free, he drew his body to hers. She relished the feel of him sliding inside. It was as if they were made for each other. Mei took him deep, only to meet his rhythm as he pulled back. With a whimper, she wound her hands into his dark hair, the locks so silky and smooth. His smell engulfed her, and his lips held traces of her taste on them.

Her heart ached even as the pleasure built inside her body. Mei wanted this moment to last forever. She pulled him closer. He thrust harder, faster, deeper, answering her body's silent cry for more. A second climax was close.

She trembled, panted, sighed for more. Tension gathered in her hips, and she knew she was close. Jarek pushed up his knee, angling her just as she liked, putting the perfect amount of pressure on her as he worked in and out. It was too much. Suddenly, she exploded, trembling with her intense climax. Closing her eyes, lights exploded beneath her lids. She squeezed him hard, causing him to come with her. His body released into hers, filling her with his seed. Breathing rapidly, he fell against her. Mei held him close, not caring that she was crushed by his weight.

"We should get dressed," he whispered. "We should be in the cockpit so you can show Lochlann where to land."

Mei nodded, letting go. Jarek seemed reluctant as he pulled away. Standing by the bed, he reached his hand out to her. She took it, and he pulled her to her feet. He kissed her softly, brushing her damp hair from her cheek.

Mei gave him a sad smile, unable to speak. He nodded in understanding, not saying anything either.

Please be wrong, grandmother. Please, I beg of you, fate, be wrong.

24

OUTSIDE THE LIN YAO MINES, SINGHAI TERRITORY, LINTIAN

JAREK GLANCED OVER AT MEI. No matter how much he'd pleaded with her to remain with the ship, she'd refused to stay behind. Unfortunately, he didn't have much room to fight with her on the matter, since she was the only one who knew the way.

Their lovemaking had left a bittersweet feeling inside his chest. He knew the honor in her and knew the risk he took in kidnapping her, but he didn't have a choice. When she had been unconscious, he'd contacted her brother. The man had naturally been upset until he told him that Mei had a message for him. He'd lied to Haun, telling him that it was part of her fate that brought her onto Jarek's ship. The Zhang prince instantly understood the words and wanted to speak directly to Mei, but Jarek pretended that he couldn't hear the request as he fiddled with the controls to break up the sound.

Jarek then promised to send the map to the palace by way of a messenger pod when they were closer to the planet. Prince Haun had demanded his sister's return. Jarek had somehow convinced him that she was safe and that she would be returned. Closing his eyes, he knew that the Var royal family seal he'd sent with the map would help to convince the man of his honor.

With what he was going to do, Jarek didn't feel like he had much honor this day.

"*Shh,*" Mei said under her breath. "Someone's coming."

Jarek glanced at her. She'd bound her hair into a bun on the back of her neck. They were lined up along a ridge, resting on their stomachs. Lucien and Lochlann were still on the ship, standing guard. If *The Conqueror* was discovered or if there was trouble in the mines, Jarek needed the two men ready to go. When he caught Mei's attention, he raised a brow.

"The wind told me," she whispered.

Jarek nodded, sniffing. She was right. Someone was coming.

Below them, a valley was covered in small purplish-red flowers spotted with even smaller blue ones. The only entrance into the mines was in the valley, beyond which were miles of rolling hills. Blades of yellow and blue grasses stretched as far as their eyes could see. A few farmhouses were clustered close together to form a village, standing out against the pale blue of the cloudless sky. Lintian truly was as close to paradise as any planet in the known galaxies. It only added to his guilt in stealing her away from it.

He forced himself not to think about it. According to Mei, the modest nearby farms were fronts for the Lin Yao Mining Corporation. There was even a full crop of giant red flowers, which grew low to the ground. The farms looked authentic, and Jarek wouldn't have been able to tell that they weren't real without her help.

A single man came out of the mines. He glanced around, shading his eyes. Then, turning back toward where he'd come from, he waved his arm. A furry, bright red creature lumbered out, led by two farmers in drab brown clothes. The beast of burden pulled a cart behind him.

"Purple jade?" Jarek asked quietly.

Mei shook her head. "No, jade is only harvested at night. It is the law. Emperor Song fears that the mine location will be photographed from space."

"With today's technology, night really doesn't

prevent that," Viktor said. "Almost any ship can photograph through darkness if they have the right equipment."

Mei smirked but said nothing.

"I'll go around," Dev said. "Evan, you come with me."

Jarek nodded in agreement. Dev and Evan backed up, making sure they were out of sight, before jogging along the ridge.

"I need to see what's on that cart," Mei said, making a move to follow Dev.

Jarek grabbed her arm and shook his head in denial. "Stay by my side. Whatever is on that cart will be inside the mines as well."

"But—"

"Don't risk yourself for what might only be mining tools or loose rocks." Jarek didn't let go, and she didn't answer. They laid in wait as the slow beast hauled the cart. When the small traveling party finally made their way down the valley and out of sight, Jarek motioned for the group to move.

Jackson led them down the narrow cliff. As the best climber, he knew just where they needed to place their feet to descend. When the man reached the bottom, he held out his hands. Viktor jumped down, catching Jackson's hands to silence his fall. Jarek followed suit, only to turn back to Mei. She had borrowed a pair of Lucien's pants. They were a little big on her, but it was the best they could do.

Jarek held his hands out for Mei. She glanced over his shoulder and pushed off the cliff. Somersaulting in the air, she landed neatly on her feet. Jarek was impressed.

"Come on," he ordered, running toward the mine's entrance. He kept his eye on the direction where the cart had disappeared. The soft flowers crushed beneath their feet. He regretted the trail it left behind, but there was no other way into the mines.

Jarek reached out with his senses. The way was clear. He pushed faster, glancing at Mei to make sure she kept up.

As they hit the mines, he saw Dev motion from a low ridge. Jarek signaled back at him. He knew that the man would come in after them, just in case there was trouble.

Stalactites and stalagmites reached like jaws from the ceilings and floors along the entranceway. Mei took the lead, slipping by Jarek before he could stop her. He hurried in after her, concentrating hard. The rock was chipped away with low burning lights strung along them. Jarek noticed a few places where black scorch marks marred the surface. The dirt floor was littered with pebbles.

The dim light of the cave was a stark contrast

to the light outside. Viktor's foot slipped. They all froze, waiting to see if anyone heard. When no alarm was sounded, they again moved deeper into the mine's long corridor.

Mei stopped as they reached a round chamber. Six tunnels fanned out from the main entrance. Taking a light, Mei tilted it up from its place on the wall. It shone over the top of the openings, showing the Lintianese symbols carved crudely over them.

"*Made!*" she swore. "Sacred cats!"

"What is it?" Jarek asked, smirking as she used his curse word.

"They're just numbers. I don't know which we should try first." Mei wiped her brow, frowning. "Beyond this there should be more tunnels. If you don't know where you're going, there is no telling where you'll end up."

"That one," Viktor said, pointing. The third cave had a barricade in front of it, blocking access. "If I was doing something illegal, I'd want to make sure the night crew wasn't coming in for a visit."

"Smart thinking," Jarek said in approval, slapping him on the back. Viktor grunted. Jarek took the opportunity to lead as he pushed past Mei. He heard her gasp lightly, but she didn't protest out loud.

Jarek ran his hands over the barricade, trying to

see the easiest way in. He wasn't exactly small like Mei's people.

"Here," Viktor said, leaning over to feel along the floor. "It should be…right…down…*ahh*." The barricade unlatched, falling back like a door. "There it is."

"How'd you know?" Mei asked, impressed.

Viktor grinned. "Misspent youth. The door had to be one piece if that cart was to fit through it."

"Good point," she said, again moving past Jarek to take the lead. Jarek frowned as he followed behind her. The tunnel was long and straight. The lights dimmed for a long run only to again light the way, better than before.

"Oh, baby cakes, don't be angry," a voice said from down the hall. It was in the star language. "Behaving is such a broad term, open to interpretation. When I said I'd behave, I didn't say how."

Jarek grabbed Mei's arm, thrusting her protectively behind him.

"Ah, sweet cheeks, you're breaking my heart," the voice continued.

"Rick," Viktor, Jackson and Jarek whispered at once. Relief curled through Jarek, unknotting his stomach, only to be replaced instantly by wariness.

"That's him?" Mei asked. "That easy?"

"I guess so," Jarek said though something didn't feel right about what was happening.

"It does feel a little too easy, captain," Viktor said. "We walk in and *poof* we find Rick just like that?"

"Frankly, honey pie, I'm disappointed in you," Rick continued. "All this time and you were so easy to catch off guard. What? Nothing to say now? No smartass command? No snide remarks?"

"Something is off," Jackson said.

Jarek took a deep breath. "Maybe we're finally hitting a patch of good luck. With everything that's gone wrong, we're about due for something to go right, wouldn't you say?"

Jackson nodded, but the motion looked reluctant.

"Jackson, go back the way we came, make sure we're not being followed," Jarek whispered. "I don't smell anyone behind us, but I'm not taking the chance."

Jackson nodded and did as he was ordered.

"Mei, you stay here with Viktor. I'm going on alone." Jarek hated having her there, but staying between him and Jackson was the safest place for her considering the circumstances.

"No, I—" she began to protest.

Viktor tugged her back when she began to follow. She glanced at the slender man, looking annoyed before nodding at Jarek.

"Be careful," she mouthed.

Jarek nodded once. He turned to where they'd heard Rick's voice. Creeping along the passageway, he let claws grow from the tips of his fingers and fangs from his gums. The light brightened, changing to an orange firelight that glowed over the dark mine walls. He felt the warmth of it on his skin.

Jarek detected two others besides Rick in the room. He heard a muffled cry and the sound of a boot sliding along the pebbled ground. Concentrating on where he heard the boot, he roared to surprise his opponents. Jumping from his hiding spot, he stood ready to battle. His arm drew back, ready to tear at a drug trader's throat.

"Holy space balls," Rick exclaimed. "Captain? Is that really you?"

Jarek blinked. His gaze darted over the room. Rick stood, hands on hips with a look of surprise on his face. Next to him was Prince Haun. He recognized Mei's brother from when he'd kidnaped her. His stomach tightened. How did the Zhang prince get there so soon? Was he in on the drug trade? If so, what was Rick doing free?

In the middle of the room was a woman tied to a chair. It took him a moment, but he recognized her as the drug trader who'd kidnaped Rick.

"Rick?" Jarek questioned. Confusion warred

with his relief that his friend was all right. "You're…free? How? I don't understand."

Rick crossed over to Jarek and grabbed him in a giant hug, laughing heartily. "Blessed stars, Jarek, it's good to see you. How did you ever find me?"

"You should've known I would," Jarek said, patting Rick hard on the back. He grabbed the man's face and shook it once before letting go. "Now, how did you get free? What is going on here? I come expecting a rescue and I see you tormenting some woman."

"Oh, yeah, sorry, cap. This is Prince Zhang Haun of the, uh, Moon Empire," Rick said, stepping back toward Prince Haun.

"Muntong," Haun corrected, his voice quipped.

"Right, right, Muntong." Rick grinned, slapping the prince on the back. The prince blinked in surprise at the familiar contact. "Anyway, ole Haun here saved my sorry ass. He said we were waiting for someone, but I never thought he meant you. I thought it was just my lucky day."

Jarek relaxed. Rick looked tired and worn. A bruise was healing on the side of his face, and he was too skinny as if starved. Even his clothes had seen better days. They hung tattered and dirty on his frame.

"Sacred cats, Rick! You need a bath." Jarek wrinkled his nose, before laughing.

"Jarek?" Mei's voice said from behind him.

Jarek tensed. Slowly he turned, and his smile faded. She stood in the entryway, and her eyes had found her brother.

"*Meimei*," Haun said, his face softening as he spoke to his sister in their native tongue. Rick looked confused. Jarek understood perfectly. "Is it really you?"

"*Gē ge*," Mei exclaimed, running forward to embrace him.

"Who's that?" Rick whispered. "His woman?"

"That is Princess Mei, his sister. We had her on our ship. She helped us to find these mines."

"Don't tell me you kidnaped her in exchange for me," Rick said in amazement. "I mean, yeah, I'm worth it but didn't you learn anything from when we kidnaped Falke?"

"What was I supposed to learn?" Jarek said, barely paying attention as he listened to Mei assure Haun that she had been treated well and was all right. She even told him that she was to blame for her disappearance.

"That people fall in love if you kidnap royalty. Just as your brother and Sam did." Rick shook his head. "But, no harm, no foul, and, thankfully," Rick glared at the prisoner tied to the chair, "no love."

Jarek frowned. Rick was quoting an odd twentieth century Earth saying again.

"What in the star blazes does that mean?" Jarek asked, his voice sharper than he intended. No one had fallen in love? Yeah, right.

"Haun, what are you doing here?" Mei asked.

"Prince Jarek tried to contact me at our home. Since he insisted on talking to me, Jin answered in my place. Prince Jarek told Jin, who later informed me, what you had discovered. He also told me of the map and how it was your fate to go on his ship to see it. All is forgiven, *meimei*. With this news, the family understands why you acted the way you did. I am happy you are safe, little sister."

Prince Jin? Jarek frowned. That was how Haun had reached the mines before them. He was already on the Singhai side of the planet.

"Please forgive my brother, Jin's, deceit but it was necessary," Haun said. Jarek nodded, not really concerned. His thoughts raced. If Haun were here, he'd want to keep Mei by his side. How was he supposed to take Mei with him if her brother was there to stop him? He couldn't hurt the prince. She would never forgive him.

She might not forgive me for stealing her away.

Jarek looked into Mei's eyes. The room was quiet. Tears built in her gaze, tearing at him. He could tell by her look that she was trying to tell him goodbye.

"What of the men who left here with a cart?" Mei asked.

"Our guards in disguise. They are taking proof of the chandoo drugs to our shores. A ship awaits their return."

"*Argh!*" the woman tied to the chair hissed. Jarek glanced over to see Rick patronizingly patting the back of her head.

"What are you going to do with her?" Jarek asked.

"I've made arrangements to take her with us for punishment," Rick said. Jarek saw something in his friend's eyes, something he'd never imagined seeing in Rick.

"I thank you for returning my sister to me, Prince Jarek," Haun said. "If you would hand over the map of my palace, all will be forgiven."

Jarek glanced at the floor. "It's on my ship. I thought it would be safer to leave it there."

Haun nodded in understanding. "Very good. Again I thank you. If you please, let us go to your ship now and retrieve it so you may be on your way."

"We're not taking them with us to the palace?" Mei gasped in surprise. Almost desperately, she hurried, "Won't father wish to meet them?"

"I'm sure Prince Jarek has many duties awaiting his attention," Haun said, his expression stern. He stared at Jarek, meeting his eyes in warning, as he reached for his sister's arm. "Come Mei. We will wait for them outside the mines. The sooner we get you home, the better I will feel."

"I owe them, Haun. We owe them. Please," Mei whispered. Jarek knew she didn't mean for him to hear her, but his Var hearing detected her words easily. "It's a matter of my honor."

"Prince Jarek, forgive me for my hasty words. Of course, you are invited to the palace. Emperor and Empress Zhang would be honored to have you as their guests."

"Mei?" Jarek asked her. Mei nodded. "We would be honored to be your guests."

Haun nodded once before leading Mei from the small, barren room. Rick hauled his prisoner up from the chair and thrust her before him.

"Come on you," Rick hissed. "Payback is going to be hell."

The woman grunted, cursing him through her gag. Rick laughed, a mocking, hard sound. Jarek wondered what exactly had happened to his carefree friend to make his manners so sinister. The woman tripped, but Rick's hold on her tied wrists kept her upright and walking.

Jarek took a deep breath, alone in the room. He

had to find a way to take Mei with him from the palace. His heart ached with the idea of leaving her. But how was he to get her away from Haun? The man didn't seem as though he would let her out of his sight for very long. Jarek could well understand. He, too, felt protective of her.

"Forgive me, Mei, for anything I might have to do," he whispered. Determined, he followed the others.

IMPERIAL PALACE OF THE ZHANG
DYNASTY, HONORABLE CITY,
MUNTONG TERRITORY, PLANET OF
LINTIAN

JAREK'S first sight of the Honorable City was the high walls blocking the palace from the outside world. A moat surrounded the walls, its waters still with what looked like long spikes peeking out from the depths. It wasn't a very welcoming sight. Vines of bluish weeds wrapped around the spikes and small, orange fish weaved in schools around them.

Since his own home overlooked the surrounding valley, he couldn't imagine being blockaded inside four walls, hidden from the surrounding landscape. He felt claustrophobic just thinking about it. At least on his ship they were heading somewhere, with endless stars all around them. The wide front gate was ornately gilded, carved with two circular dragon patterns with symbols down the side. They slowly crept open as two guards allowed them entrance.

Beyond the gate, the lavish hidden world of Honorable City awaited them. Jarek glanced back at the lush countryside. Mei's homeland was a true paradise amongst planets. As they'd flown over the planet in their ship, navigating over the plains as they flew through the pale blue sky, they'd seen a few farmhouses that were clustered close together to form a village, and a large forest with strange spiny leaf covered trees. Fields of giant, red flowers contrasted against the blades of the yellowish-blue grasses.

Inside the palace walls, pathways led through the landscaped complex. Everything was neat and tidy, even the plant life. He didn't see one dried blossom or dying leaf on any of it. Barren torches lined the walkway. Jarek knew they didn't have the aid of moonlight on Lintian, and the torches would be necessary to light the grounds. Mei's family used natural elements for light, as opposed to computer operated systems.

Even though the buildings looked complex in decor, there was a simplicity to the design of the palace grounds. From the map, he knew they were laid out in a giant rectangle, with many buildings for different functions—from an archery range to barracks for the imperial guards. There was also a small creek that flowed within the walls. It was a little city made solely for the pleasure of the royal family.

Mei had ridden across the Satlyun River by ship with her brother, as Jarek flew with his crew back into space, only to wait for the Zhang prince to arrive safely at Muntong's shores. When they reached the docks, Mei cleared them for landing, and they reentered the atmosphere to join the Zhang royals. Rick's prisoner provided the crew with mild entertainment and speculation, especially since they'd never seen a woman infuriate Rick as much as she did. He called her wench most of the time, along with several other choice names, but they all highly doubted any of them were her real name.

Though, it turned out to be as they'd suspected all along, the woman was a drug trader, and Rick had been in the wrong place at the wrong time. While in pursuit, and not taking no for an answer, Rick had followed the woman into a private hall. Her comrades had shown themselves, and he was taken prisoner. While in captivity, he was put in the woman's care, though she wasn't much of a caretaker. Jarek wondered if spending several weeks tied to a chair would make Rick more cautious. Somehow, he highly doubted it. The oddest part of the whole ordeal was that when the woman looked at Rick, though there was a lot of anger, there was something else in her too. Whatever it was, Evan was steering clear, wanting no part of it.

Seeing Mei looking at him brought Jarek back to the moment. He hadn't been alone with her since before they had gone into the mines. Giving her a soft smile, he resisted the urge to go to her. She was beautiful, dressed in silk like the Lintianese princess she was. His heart ached with the need to hold her, and his body yearned to make love to her. The pain was so bad, he was sure he'd die from a broken heart if he were to leave her behind. He had missed her terribly during their time apart.

But how can I take her from this paradise? What do I offer her? Space? Dirty fuel ports and endless nights flying through stars with no one but the crew for company?

Guilt and heartache warred within him, and he lost some of his resolve to kidnap her. Jarek couldn't help but stare, ignoring the beautiful palace as they walked beneath that gate.

What do I do? I can't leave her. Sacred cats, I can't.

Haun looked down at his sister, drawing Mei's attention away from Jarek.

"Look at those," Evan whispered at his side. The man was talking to Jackson, but Jarek followed his finger anyway. Strange pink flowers lined the paths, interwoven with others that were shaped like an eight-point, dark blue star with a golden center. Tiny winged creatures fluttered over the petals. Their bodies were so small compared to their large black wings. The shape of the number '7' formed when their wings bent forward in flight.

"Well, would you kiss my comet, cap," Rick said. "Will you look at this place? It's a pretty sweet setup they have going here. I could get into this."

The man was a little too loud and drew the attention of Mei and Haun. Mei tried not to laugh, Haun's lips pressed tightly together in censure.

"Do not get into anything," Jarek ordered under his breath. "Don't make me regret taking you along, or saving your ass."

"Sure thing, homey," Rick nodded.

"Stop talking," Jarek ordered, not understanding the man's word. Sometimes he thought Rick just pretended to be into twentieth century Earth memorabilia, and really just made things up as he went along. He'd be convinced of it, if not for the numerous times he'd caught the man with contraband old movie transmissions.

The Honorable City was a beautiful place, with attention paid to every detail—from the curved roofs that pointed up toward the heavens to the mosaic pathways that led to a few of the sacred buildings. Mei dropped behind her brother to walk next to Jarek.

"I miss you," she said quietly.

Jarek felt like he could breathe again at her admittance. "As I you, *fea*."

"What do you think of the palace?" she asked.

Jarek couldn't take his eyes off her. "Beautiful."

She blushed and glanced around. "Haun is taking you to be introduced to my family. They're waiting for us in the Hall of Infinite Wisdom. If you could, please keep Rick from talking…" Her tone dropped off as she gave the man in question a wary glance. "It's not that I don't like him, but his words are not appropriate for my parents' company."

"Consider it done," Jarek said. Turning to Rick, he told him, "Utter a word to the emperor or his wife and you'll never get planet leave again."

Rick paled and nodded. No planet leave for Rick meant no womanly company.

"Thank you," Mei said. "They're very old-fashioned and wouldn't find him as humorous as I do. They might actually lock him in the prisons."

"I agree, avoiding an incident is for the best." Jarek's stomach knotted. He'd fought men and creatures without thought, outrun imperial guards and stolen maps from impenetrable fortresses, but just the idea of meeting Mei's parents made him tenser than any of their other antics.

Mei touched his arm briefly, letting her fingers

curl around his bicep before letting go of him. She smiled, her eyes showing her longing to hold him. It was almost as intense as his desire for her. Dropping her hand, she turned toward a building. The Hall of Infinite Wisdom was located in the center of the compound. It was the largest structure they'd seen so far, set high upon stone, and towering over the surrounding courtyard and gardens. Like all the buildings, it had yellow tiled roofs and dark red walls.

"This is it," she whispered. Jarek detected her shaking. Mei hardly ever showed fear, so what was this nervousness now?

Haun led them inside the hall. Jarek's crew got quiet. Rick walked between Lochlann and Evan, his mouth tightly shut as if he was afraid he'd speak. Jarek hid a smile. The two men looked ready to grab him and haul him back if it became necessary.

Lucien and Viktor had stayed back with the ship to guard the prisoner. Someone needed to stay with the ship, and they'd drawn the wrong lot. Dev walked behind all of them, keeping guard at their backs. Jarek knew he was watching closely for an attack. Partly because they didn't know this empire and thought the Zhang emperor might try to subdue those who had taken possession of his palace map, and partly because that was just the way Dev was. After years of being ridiculed and feared as a demon, he was used to people trying to attack him without reason or provocation. The sad thing was, it wasn't just non-Belvons who distrusted him. Because of Dev's mixed heritage, the Belvons had persecuted him as well. Jackson hung back, keeping Dev company.

As they walked inside, Jarek noticed that Mei distanced herself slightly from him, making sure there was space between their bodies. He wanted nothing more than to bow to her parents and proclaim her as his life mate. His crew would help him run away with her, no questions asked.

With that thought swirling in his head, Jarek's gaze darted around the hall, not really seeing anything as he searched for the emperor and empress.

You've met royalty before, he assured himself. *You are royalty, and you have done them a great service in finding the drug traders in their rival's mines. You have every right to expect appreciation.*

Yeah, and I've also been bedding their daughter for weeks now. Parents don't always look favorably on that fact.

Jarek took a deep breath, feeling like a Var child on the first day of warrior training under the imposing Commander Falke. Though, he'd much rather face a thousand commanding brothers in battle simulation, than upset the two petite, almost frail, looking people before him.

The Zhang emperor and empress sat on high thrones above the hall. Carved golden dragons coiled around the royal couple. The emperor had a long mustache that hung down the front of his tunic. They wore matching yellow embroidered silk robes decorated with imperial red dragons and ancient symbols. Since he'd seen the symbol carved on almost every surface, Jarek assumed it was either the family name or the character for royalty.

"Mei!" The empress stood, coming quickly down the platform to her daughter. Mei hurried forward and took her mother's hands. The empress looked over her daughter's shoulder to Jarek and his crew, her expression grateful. "I thank you for caring for my daughter, Prince Jarek of the Var, and for your service to the Zhang Dynasty."

"It was our pleasure to be of service, Empress," Jarek bowed at the waist.

The empress smiled and reached a hand to her daughter's cheek. She whispered something and kissed Mei's forehead before letting go of her.

"Emperor," Mei bowed her head to her father, before holding out her hand to gesture behind her. "May I present, Prince Jarek of the Var and his crew —Rick, Evan, Lochlann, Jackson, and Dev. It was their hospitality and aid that allowed me to fulfill fate's plan and discover the drug traders within the Lin Yao Mines. They are also the ones who discovered the map that Haun now possesses. We owe them all greatly for the service and kindness bestowed upon us, and I ask that you honor them as they have honored me."

"Your service to the empire is noted and appreciated," the emperor answered, bowing his head though he didn't get up from his seat.

"Prince Jarek," Mei said, turning to him. "May I present to you my family, Emperor Zhang, the Empress," she motioned to her siblings in turn, drawing his attention to them, "Prince Jin, Prince Lian, Princess Fen and Prince Shen."

Each royal family member bowed their head as their name was called. Jin stared at him the longest, a slight smile curling the side of his mouth. Jarek wondered about the look. In an odd way, the man reminded him of his brother, Falke, at least the way Falke had been before he married Samantha. Jin wasn't militant in nature like Falke was, but he was collected. There was something in his eyes, a seriousness or a burden. It was hard to put his finger on.

"My family is in your debt for your great service, and we would like to present you with the golden dragon," the empress said. Prince Lian turned and lifted a yellow pillow from a table behind him. Extending his arms, he presented the tiny figurine.

"I accept your gift on behalf of my crew," Jarek answered, taking the figurine and giving it the proper amount of attention. He'd been to enough ceremonies to be able to figure out what was happening. Turning, he handed the item to Lochlann to hold.

The empress whispered to her daughter, and Mei nodded. Mei motioned for Jarek and his crew to follow as she walked from the hall. Once outside, she let loose a long sigh. "I think you impressed them."

The men nodded, returning her look.

"That's it?" Rick asked. "Huh. That was simple."

"You kept your mouth shut," Lochlann teased. "There was nothing simple about that."

"You have no idea," Rick said. "Did you see… Uh, Mei, is your sister single?"

"Don't even think about it," Jarek ordered. The guys laughed, and Rick grumbled.

"Fen is too sweet for you, Rick," Mei said. "She'd probably bore you."

"Sweets never bore me," Rick assured her.

"No," Jarek affirmed.

"Come on, Rick," Lochlann said. "Let's think

of a plan to get you back to the Galaxy Playmates' mansion."

"There probably won't be any more mansion trips," Rick grumbled as the men pulled him away from where Mei and Jarek stood in front of the Hall of Infinite Wisdom. "Look at him. He's in *love*. Now we're not going to have any fun."

"Ah, man," Jackson said. "You can't think of it like that."

"Yeah," Lochlann assured him. "It just means that there will be more ladies for us."

Mei laughed softly, shaking her head at their conversation, as she directed her attention to Jarek. "My mother has instructed me to feed you before you leave. And they offer any supplies you might need to repair your ship. When I was with Haun, I communicated with them and told them everything that had happened."

"Everything?" he asked, trying to smile. The look failed. He was too sad.

"No, not *everything*. I would not tell them that, *qin ài de*. You would not want to lose certain parts of your anatomy, would you?"

"Would they really punish me in such a way?" Jarek bent over, and his hand moved in a protective gesture over his balls. Though, for Mei's touch, he'd gladly risk life and limb—even that special limb.

"No, not really," she said. "They know such things happen between a man and woman."

"And somehow, I see you as too wild of a flower for them to keep tame, *fea*."

"Like the wind." A tear slipped from her eye. She blinked, as if trying to keep them back, but more only spilled over her lids.

Jarek moved, so her back was to the men, hoping to save her any embarrassment. He noticed the men stepped away from them and was grateful for the privacy. "I don't want to go, Mei. I want to be with you forever. I will be your servant just to be near you. I will live here."

"You would give up space for me?" she sniffed.

"I would give up eternity for you, my love. Sweet *fea*, I would give my life for just a second more of you." Jarek's hand balled into a fist. Not touching her was torture. "Just say the words, I beg you. Tell me what I have to do to be with you. I will do anything. Please, don't make me go. Don't make me leave you behind. I don't think I can do it."

"I wish there was a way, Jarek. I truly do. But..." Mei took a deep breath, reaching forward to grab Jarek's hands in hers. "You know what I must do. I promise you, Jarek, there will not be a day that goes by when I don't think of you. But this is so much more than us. Fate has seen me with Lok. To defy that wish would be to bring disaster to my homeland. I cannot be responsible for that. I cannot. I cannot. Please, don't ask me to because I don't know if I am strong enough to do what I must."

"Will you not even try?" he pleaded. "Present me to them as your—"

"As my lover? We are not so prudish, but neither are my parents so understanding of those things, for they are still parents." Mei closed her eyes, and more tears slid in long trails down her face, wetting the front of her silk gown. "I'm sorry, Jarek. My place is here. My duty is here. I cannot forsake it. I would never forgive myself. And my greatest fear is that in time I would come to resent you for it as well."

"I've been thinking of how I was going to kidnap you and take you with me by force," Jarek admitted.

"You can't."

"I know. But, I love you too much, *fea*. You are it for me. You are my life mate."

"Jarek, no," Mei gasped. "You can't do that. You… No. You'll not have anyone else. I don't want you to live alone forever because of me. I don't want you dying of a broken heart. Please… No. I don't ask that of you. I can't ask it of you."

"I'm sorry, *fea*. It is already done. It's been done. I can't take it back. My body knows its mate, and you are it. All I want is you." Jarek pulled her to him. Her mouth turned up willingly, and she kissed him passionately. Mei's tongue fought with his as they desperately clung to each other.

"Uh..."

The sound didn't register in his mind. Mei was in his arms, and he couldn't let go.

"Cap?" Rick hissed only to say more forcibly, "Captain Jarek!"

Jarek pulled Mei closer. *Just a moment more. Please, just let me hold her a little longer. Sweet fate, if you are going to take her from me, please just give me this last moment in her arms before I have to say goodbye.*

"Zhang Mei!"

The horrified yell was enough to jolt him back. Jarek blinked heavily, looking over Mei's head. It took a stunned moment to assess what was happening. Mei's kiss was on his lips, but so were her legs wrapped around his waist. In horror, he realized her parents were staring back at him. Turning his gaze to Mei, he saw that she was a little slower in coming to her senses.

"Mei," he whispered, not knowing how to proceed. She clung desperately to him like she would never let go. Her face was still wet from tears, and he tasted the salt from them on his lips, felt the moisture of them drying on his cheek.

Mei gasped as Jarek said her name, sliding

down off his body. He shifted his weight, trying to hide his erection. It was no use. He'd worn his best pair of slacks which also happened to be a tighter pair. There was no hiding what he felt for Mei. Even without the mass between his thighs, he was sure they'd see the love in him for her. He hoped they would. He prayed to her fates, to his gods, to gods he didn't even know about, that it would be so.

"Zhang Mei," the empress repeated. Mei's face paled, and she rubbed her hands over her eyes, drying them, before turning around to face her parents. She bowed her head. The royal siblings were behind the empress, watching their sister intently. The emperor glared at Jarek from the empress' side. "What are you doing?"

"Please," Jarek said, moving to stand protectively in front of his lover. "This is my doing. Don't blame—"

"Prince Jarek. Though we said we appreciate your service to the Zhang Dynasty," the emperor said. "We did not mean that to imply you could take whatever you wish as a reward for—"

"Emperor, please," Mei pleaded. "It's my fault as well. Jarek is my..." She hesitated, looking up at him. Very softly, she finished, "He's my lover."

The empress gasped. Haun didn't move, but he did stare at his sister with an incalculable expression. The emperor's eyes narrowed on Jarek. Princess Fen smiled slightly, hiding it behind her hand as she leaned into Prince Shen's shoulder. Prince Lian thoughtfully watched over them all, neither approving nor condemning as he seemed to contemplate what was happening.

"Mei?" the empress managed, her voice trembling in apparent confusion.

"I said he is my lover," Mei repeated, moving closer to Jarek's side. She took up his hand. "And I love him. He is my heart. Emperor, please." She paused before adding, "Father, I love him."

"But, Prince Lok," the emperor said. "Your fate."

"Mei," the empress took a step forward. "Please consider what you do. I know the Songs are not what you would have, but this is not just about us. It's about Lintian. It's about our people and how we can best serve them." She motioned to Jarek. "This match has nothing to offer your future as a Zhang princess."

"We don't know that," Prince Jin said. "I think we should listen to what Mei has to say."

The empress shot him a stern look. When she turned, he tried to give his sister a reassuring smile behind their mother's back.

"I speak not of my future as a Zhang princess. I speak of my future as a woman. I know my duty," she said. Her hand shook in his and Jarek desperately wanted to pull her into his protective embrace. "And I know I must sacrifice love for duty. I know what is being asked of me. But when you speak of this… When you say… Father? Please, I love him. Can we not consider…"

"Emperor, please, hear us out. The knowledge I have of the universe could not be gained by staying on my home planet of Qurilixen. Mei can still be loyal to her family and not live within the palace, just as I am in service to my people. They depend upon my knowledge of the universe, and this knowledge I will gladly pledge in service to your empire. I humbly ask for your daughter's life, a life spent with mine, as my true wife, my mate. And I will swear on the souls of my ancestors that I will give her my life. I will take care of her and protect her. And, if ever you need us, all you have to do is call, and we will come." Jarek stared earnestly at them, hoping they would see his honest heart for what it was.

"You speak well, Prince Jarek," the emperor said, nodding. "But you are not her fate. It has been seen. It is out of our hands."

"Forgive me for arguing, but could it not be that I am her fate? That she was put on my ship to find me, as well as the map and the drug traders?" Jarek touched Mei's shoulder in support.

"If it helps, nowhere does it say in the scrolls that what the ancestors tell us is necessarily fated. Not that I believe great-grandmother is wrong, but shouldn't we consider there might be other options," Jin inserted.

"Jin, I know you mean well, and I know you are connected to our past, but this is about Mei." The empress again gave him a stern look.

"I say this not only for Mei, Empress, but for all of your children's futures." Jin took a step forward. "I would not see any have to give up their heart for the sake of honor. You know I honor the traditions, keep them, and I would give my life for the empire. But, if Mei has found her heart then——"

"It has been decided," the emperor interrupted his son. "Prince Jarek, that your proposal is sincere I have no doubt, but this..." He motioned as if that was the end of it.

"This has not been decided by us," the empress said, picking up where her husband left off, "but by fate. Fate has chosen Prince Lok for you, my daughter."

"Your place is with the father of your baby!"

Jarek jolted in surprise at the intruder's voice. He turned, shaken to see a transparent figure had joined them on the Hall of Infinite Wisdom's front steps. The womanly spirit was dressed in a Lintianese gown though the style wasn't exactly like the mortal women before him. Her long sleeves drifted behind her as the breeze swept her body forward, blowing her long, dark hair streaked with white around her head.

"An apparition," Lochlann mumbled.

"No, it's a ghost," Jackson said.

"Yeah, that's what I said," Lochlann returned.

"Holy space balls," Rick swore. He reached forward, trying to poke his finger into the transparent woman. She turned to look at him, her brow arched in surprise at his daring. Every one of her movements was silent, like the breeze. Rick didn't seem fazed by her look as he ran his hand into her upper leg. "She feels like air." He made a move to do it again, and the spirit glided out of his reach.

"This is my great-grandmother, Zhang An. She is my ancestor who helps to watch over and guide us," Mei said to Jarek. She quickly introduced the spirit to the others, not taking the care she had done when introducing her father to them. Jarek nodded, not sure what to say to the spirit.

"Grandmother," the empress said, "we can handle this."

"Mm," An answered, drifting past the empress. She sounded unsure of the woman's claim.

"Great-grandmother," Mei said. "I have heard your predictions, and I know why Prince Song Lok must be my husband. I understand now that my marriage will bring peace to our world and will help cement the relations between our two nations. With what we have discovered, I know that my marriage will mend what has been done."

"I said all that?" An snorted, the sound very unladylike.

"Yes, you said you consulted all the powers," Mei insisted. "Can't you remember? You said you did the oracle bones, the divining basin, even listened to the wind. You said you saw my fate. Please, don't you remember?"

"I did all those things, but I never said you were to marry Prince Lok. I said the first foreign man of royal blood whose path you crossed would be both father of your child and husband to you. You and your father decided on Prince Lok. I did not."

"Blessed stars," Rick mumbled, "Even her voice is airy. Jackson, you have to feel her. I swear, it's like she'd not even there, but she is."

"But," Mei stepped toward the woman, ignoring Rick. Jarek didn't bother with the man. His ears strained to hear everything that was being said between the spirit and Mei. This was his future they were talking about, his heart. He didn't have time to worry about Rick getting his ass thrown in prison if he insulted the Zhang emperor. There would be time for that later. "Prince Lok was the first man of non-Zhang royal blood to cross my path. Our marriage will ensure peace. It makes sense."

"Your place is with the father of your child," An insisted, her words slow and careful.

"I know that. I know I will bear him a child." Mei gave Jarek a forlorn look of regret and mouthed so the rest of them couldn't see, "I'm sorry you have to hear this, my love."

He shook his head, not wishing her to worry about him. Although, the thought of another man's child in her womb tormented him greatly.

"Grandmother?" the empress demanded. "Stop speaking in riddles. Out with it. If you know something you are not saying, say it now."

"What riddles? Who is speaking in riddles? I was quite clear," An huffed. "I said the first foreign man of royal blood whose path she crossed."

"And that was Prince Lok," the empress interrupted. "Mei went there with Haun, and they negotiated the exploration of the Lin Yao Mines."

"No, that was the first prince she *saw*. The first path she crossed belonged to this man, this *ten nai*, this tiger man." An turned to him. "You were in the city beyond the mountain palace, where you not? You walked the streets before you saw Mei, before Mei saw the Song prince."

Jarek nodded. "I did walk the streets."

"There, you see. He walked in one place. Mei then walked over where he had walked. She crossed his path." An grinned. "I find it a pretty simple explanation. There is no riddle in what I said."

Mei's rounded gaze turned to him. Jarek felt hope rising in his chest. If An wasn't transparent, he would have grabbed her in a hug. The woman smiled over the living, clearly savoring her moment of brilliance.

"How do you know?" the empress demanded. The emperor came to her side, touching her arm. The gesture didn't stop her. "You have no way of knowing whose path she crossed. You speak nonsense, old woman. Leave my daughter be. This decision is for the living. It's bad enough that you wanted to send her across the Satlyun, but what you say now... How will... Where will she... You would send her to the stars where we can't protect her? See her?"

The emperor pulled his wife's arm, and she looked helplessly at him. Jarek felt a sting as the woman openly rejected his suit of Mei.

"I know," An declared. "Besides, she should marry the father of her unborn child."

It took Jarek a moment to realize what was being said. Mei gasped, her hand flying to her stomach. The steps became deadly quiet for a long time as they all stared at Mei.

"My love?" he said softly, touching her stomach. "*Fea*?"

Mei bit her lip, looking as stunned as he was. Pleasure filled him at the thought. Mei with his child! Surely her parents could not protest their marriage now.

"Way to go, cap!" Rick yelled suddenly, breaking the awkward silence. "You sent off some straight shooters right up the old—"

"Rick," Dev growled, reaching to grab the man and shut him up. He shook him violently, jolting him like a rag doll.

"Ow, let go," Rick cried. Dev released him. "I didn't knock her up."

"You insolent little..." An began, turning on Rick.

"Whoa, easy there, ghostly sweetness," Rick said, grinning at the older woman. "You'll get your chance at me. No need to call Dev names."

An's figure shuddered with light and her face tinted with the lightest of pinks. Furious, she pointed at him, "I will teach you respect, little man. You will bow in the presence of my greatness."

Rick paled. "Hey, now, I was just joking around. Things were getting a little tense, and I was just trying to save the captain from everyone's anger. You know, lightening the mood with humor."

"Do not make me curse you," An warned.

"Rick, I'd listen to her and say no more," Evan said.

"Easy, don't get your, uh, gown in a twist," Rick said, ignoring Evan's sensible words. "No need to threaten us with whatever mojo power thing you have."

"What does that mean? Twisting gown?" Mei whispered. Jarek shrugged, not knowing.

"Ah, so you think you are funny," An said. "Let's see how humorous you and your friends think my power is."

The crew glared at Rick for getting them in trouble with the spirit. Jackson hit his arm. An's eyes glazed over with white. Jarek took a step forward to protect his men. Mei pulled him back, shaking her head.

"She predicts their future. No physical harm will come to them," she assured him.

"Together you travel, and together you'll remain. Tied and joined like the five elements of our people." An's voice took on an ominous quality. "The road to happiness is very rocky for all of you."

"What does that mean?" Lochlann whispered.

"Is she telling the truth?" Jackson questioned.

"I don't know," Evan said. "I can't read spirits."

"Great going, space cadet," Jackson nudged Rick.

An's eyes cleared, and she smiled vindictively, clearly knowing something they all didn't. "You will find your love hidden within the mystery of the five elements. One element for each of you. The corresponding element will hold the secret to your future happiness. But fate is not clear. If you do not recognize it, you will lose it and be forever alone."

"Elements?" Lochlann uttered. All five of the crewmen looked horrified and enraptured at the same time. "What elements?"

"Yes. The secret of your future is hidden in the five elements—metal, water, wood, earth and fire." The ghostly ancestor grinned wickedly.

"Which one am I?" Jackson asked.

"And I?" Lochlann questioned.

"That is for you to figure out." With that, An disappeared, blowing away on a sudden gust of wind.

"How does predicting what will come curse us?" Rick asked, frowning in confusion.

"She just gives us enough to consume our thoughts," Evan said. "Trust me, knowing only a very small piece of something will drive you mad. The thought will creep into our heads and make us crazy."

"Metal, wood..." Lochlann began, frowning.

"Water, earth, fire," Evan finished.

"Dev's got fire, that's easy," Rick said. "And I must be metal because my body is rock hard with muscles."

"I think the elements refer to the ones we are meant for," Evan said. "Not who we are."

"She didn't say that," Rick protested. "I'm metal, I know it."

Seeing his men were unharmed, Jarek turned to Mei and touched her stomach. He was so happy. Nothing could bring him greater joy. His princess carried his child.

"Mei," he whispered, awed. His heart soared with hope.

"Jarek," she said. "*Qin ài de!*"

"No," the empress denied. "Mei, please, reconsider."

"It is her choice," the emperor decreed. "Zhang An is right. We assumed she meant Prince Lok. If this is not so, we cannot deny Prince Jarek anymore than we could have denied Song Lok. Haun has said the Song prince showed no interest in her as a wife. Fate has willed it and it appears as if our daughter has accepted her true fate. She has accepted Prince Jarek of the Var."

"Mei?" The empress stepped forward, her face pleading.

"I choose Prince Jarek," she said, grinning up at

him. Jarek yelled, unable to contain his happiness as he picked her up and swung her in his arms. Mei kissed him, moaning that she loved him into his mouth as he spun her in a circle.

When he set her down, the empress said, "You are going to leave us, my little one, aren't you? The day you were born, Mei, I knew that you would be the one to leave us as soon as I looked into your eyes for the first time. When I heard that your future was with Song Lok, I was happy that it was not as bad as I feared. Across the Satlyun would keep you close to us, closer than the stars."

Mei let go of him and went to her mother. "I will come back. I promise."

Haun was the first sibling to come forward. "Mei has always been like the wind, and we have kept her trapped for too long. Prince Jarek speaks wisely. To understand what is out there will only make our reign more secure. Her knowledge will help us in the future. It must be so. Fate has chosen wisely."

A tear slipped over Mei's face. Jarek stayed back, letting her have a moment with her family. He motioned his crew to leave. They did quietly, still stunned by what had happened with Zhang An. Evan was right. Already Jarek could see the questions on their faces. Later, they'd be punishing Rick for making the spiteful prediction happen.

"Congratulations, *meimei*," Haun said to his sister. There was an air of sadness to him, but he nodded once at Jarek. "You have made a fine choice."

At his words, the other Zhang siblings rushed forward.

"Yes, Mei," Fen said, tearing up. "But I will miss you. You must send transmissions often. Promise? And make sure you include pictures so that I may see what you see."

"I will," Mei said.

"The palace will not be the same without you." Fen grabbed her, hugging her tightly.

"Ah, little one," Shen said when his sisters parted. He grinned, hugging Mei before stepping aside.

"Many blessings, sister," Lian said. "I believe fate has done well for you."

"Yes, many blessings," Jin added.

Lian reached for Jarek, shaking his hand. It prompted the other brothers to do the same. Jarek clasped their palms in his, nodding gratefully for their support because he knew it would mean a lot to Mei to have her family behind her decision. And if she were happy, it would mean a lot to him as well.

The emperor came forward, looking down at her stomach before slowly nodding. "This is always your home, Mei. I, like the others, have known that you would someday leave us. Your eyes have always been turned away from this place, and your spirit has always been too free to confine within the palace walls. Go with my blessing."

"*Xièxie nî*," Mei said. "Thank you."

"But, you do not need to leave us yet," the empress said in a rush. "There is no reason why you can't stay for a wedding. It would be wise to do it quickly because of the baby."

"We are already a little married," Mei said, quickly adding, as her mother frowned, "in Jarek's culture. It's called life mating, and it is very binding."

Mei looked back at him and smiled.

The empress looked at her husband.

"We will say she was married by foreign custom," Emperor Zhang said. "That way there will be no talk of the baby being created before its time. It will save any scandal."

"But they must still make an offering," Mei's mother insisted. The emperor nodded in agreement.

"Prince Jarek, please accept our hospitality for you and your crew. There is no reason to run off right away." The empress touched her daughter's cheek. "We will have a banquet to honor your marriage and to recognize you as our son."

"I would be honored." Jarek didn't care where he was, as long as Mei was his. And she was. She was his wife.

"Come," the emperor ordered, making his family leave. "Lian, go and find where Prince Jarek's crew has gone. Invite them to dine with us."

Lian did as he was ordered. The others left at the emperor's prompting.

When they were alone, Mei squealed and jumped into his arms. "I never dreamed that I could be so happy, *qin ài de*. I…"

Her words trailed off as she kissed him, wrapping her legs around his waist.

"Ah, *fea*," Jarek growled. "I've missed being alone with you, wife."

"Wife?" she repeated softly as if awed by the word. "I like you calling me that."

"Ah, sweet, beautiful *fea*." He lightly kissed the tip of her nose. "I love you more than there are stars in the galaxies."

Mei smiled, her whole heart shining in her expression as she looked at him. To Jarek, Mei was perfection. Leaning in for a kiss, she whispered against his mouth, "And I love you an infinity past that, my pirate husband."

VAR PALACE, PLANET OF QURILIXEN

Two Months Later...

Mei took a deep breath as the docking plank slowly lowered on Jarek's home planet of Qurilixen. They were outside the Var palace, literally on the bottom of a long row of steps leading to the back entrance. After spending time with her family, they'd finally left Lintian so she could meet his. Though she was nervous about meeting his family, he'd assured her quite thoroughly that they would love her. Already he'd told her of some of their customs, which helped to prepare her.

Mei glanced at Jarek as he neared, holding out his arm. The crew was still onboard, shutting down all the systems. Her cat-shifting husband was excited to be home and had been too anxious to be of much help to them. Just seeing his pleasure intensified her own.

When she had dressed that morning, Mei wasn't sure what to wear and had gone through almost every stitch of clothing. Jarek wore a tight tank shirt with cross laces down the side from under the arm to his hip. His pants were the same style, showing peeks of flesh as the cross laces worked down his hip over his upper thigh. The material was soft, not like silk, but a fuzzier soft that made her want to press her face to his chest and cuddle. With the combination of her overly excited pregnancy hormones and his sexiness, Mei had him out of his clothes and on the bed within seconds.

After they'd made love, Jarek had helped her pick a simple red and black dragon silk gown that she tied around her waist forming a low-slung skirt, along with one of Viktor's better linen shirts. The slender man's clothing fit her better than anything else that was available. She wasn't as nicely dressed as she would've liked, but Jarek assured her she was beautiful.

Mei looked around. Qurilixen was hardly like Lintian in landscape or in style. Whereas Lintian had a civil elegance, Qurilixen had an untamed feel —from the tall palace to the forest with overlarge foliage, to the fact that the entire planet consisted mostly of virile male shifters. Even the air seemed to fill her with excitement and energy, which pumped in her blood, exciting her whole system.

"It smells so sweet," she said. "And I suddenly feel as if I have a ton of energy."

"The blue sun," Jarek answered, pointing toward the blue-green sky. The unique hue of the planet's atmosphere was due to the three suns, two yellow and one blue. They cast the planet in constant daylight, with the exception of one night a year when everything aligned perfectly, and darkness fell over the land. "Remember I told you only about one in a million of Qurilixian births are female?"

Mei nodded.

"It is because of the blue sun. Its radiation gives us a long life and vitality. Over the generations, it has altered our genetics, so we create only strong, large boys." He smiled, touching her stomach. "Like our son. I believe that your visit here will be good for you and him."

"I don't want him getting too big," Mei protested, her thighs clamping shut automatically at the thought. "Not until he comes out."

Jarek laughed. Mei didn't think it was too funny, but let it pass. There would be plenty of time to worry about the size of Jarek's child inside of her.

A breeze stirred around her, making her shiver with a chill. Mei smiled, closing her eyes.

"Do you hear something?" Jarek asked in full acceptance of her gifts.

"It says everything will be fine with this birth," she said.

"Mm, good wind," he said, pulling her closer. "Does it say anything else?"

"Um," Mei twisted her mouth in thought. "That you're the sexiest man it's ever seen."

"Really?" He gave her a cocky grin.

"Mm-hmm." She lifted up on her toes to give him a kiss. Jarek slid his arm around her back and held her steady, supporting her weight. With a light sound of contentment, she pulled back when he deepened the kiss. "When I told you that I was easily excited these days, I wasn't kidding. If you want to see your family anytime today, you'll stop doing that."

Jarek groaned but pulled back. Offering his arm, he led her up the stairs. Mei tried to focus on the landscape, anything to take her mind, and her hands, off her gorgeous husband.

The forest, which Jarek had asked Rick to fly over so she could see it, was gigantic in size. The trees were so big around they looked about half the thickness of Jarek's ship. When he told her his twin brother Reid had built a house within one of the trees, she wasn't surprised. Their red bark was an interesting shade, one she'd never seen before in plant life. Yellow ferns dotted the ground, contrasting with the red dirt of the planet's surface.

Closer to the palace, the yellow fern didn't grow, but it seemed the stone that constructed the palace had. The castle-like structure stretched high into the sky, with tall pillars and square turrets that reached up into the blue-green heavens. She lost sight of some of it as they walked down the plank to the bottom of the stairwell. Jarek held her arm, walking extra slow.

Her husband was really protective now that she'd started to show in her pregnancy. It was just a little swell, but it made him nervous about her well-being all the same. Mei refused to put up with his constant over-protective streak. Every time he made her mad, she'd just disappear into the grates in *The Conqueror's* ceiling. It would take a while, but she planned on exploring the whole area. Already, she'd found some fascinating things up there, like an antique taser that had to be at least a hundred years old, and a woman's shoe. None of the men had seen the style before and by the layer of dust caking it, it had to be old.

"What do you think?" he asked.

"Not bad for a bunch of tiger men," she said, grinning.

"We're not all tigers."

"Oh?" Mei asked in surprise. "Do you mean the dragon-shifters? You have them here as well? I thought you didn't get along with them too well."

"No, the Draig own the northern half of the planet. We rule the southern section. The Draig are all dragons, but we Var are cat-shifters. Reid and I are tigers. Quinn is a cougar, Kirill is a black panther, and Falke is a white tiger. It's really a toss-up about what kind of cat a child will become."

"When do they usually shift for the first time?" Mei asked, suddenly realizing what was inside her. Though, if the baby looked like his father and had his traits, it wouldn't make any difference to her.

"Within the first year. Each child is different, and normally the shifts are for small periods of time. They're really adorable, though, just ornery little balls of fur."

Mei laughed. As long as they didn't come out like that, she'd be all right.

When they finally made it to the top, Mei smiled as she looked up. A long, wide walkway led to the Var palace. It looked as high as the Honorable City was long. Artfully, getting out of Jarek's hold, she hurried to the railing to better see the city they'd passed before landing. It stretched out in a valley beyond the front palace gate. The homes were constructed of gray bricks, contrasting to the red earthen streets, which were formed like a bustling maze throughout the village. Stunning woven rugs and blankets hung outside in the sun, drying on lines. Clay pots sat outside doorsteps, some with flowers and other native plants. The walls were decorated with tiles.

"Mei," Jarek said from her side. "Come, meet my family."

She turned in time to see a man as large as Dev coming out of the palace door. Only this man had tanned brown skin, not red. Every inch of him bulged with muscles, from his thick arms to his broad shoulders, his hands, his chest. He didn't smile when he looked at them. The rigid size of him gave her pause, and she moved closer to her husband.

Jarek hurried forward, pulling her by her arm. "Mei, this is Falke, Commander of the Guard, leader of the Var military."

"Falke," Mei said, bowing her head. "I have heard many things about you."

"Falke, this is Mei," Jarek paused. "My wife."

"Wife?" Falke asked, a smile spreading over his face. It instantly changed his appearance. "You did not tell us of a wife!"

"I wanted to surprise you," Jarek said.

Falke laughed. "You're just in time for a surprise of your own. Jasmine is giving birth."

"Now?" Jarek asked. Falke nodded. "When we got the call that you were coming, they sent me to get you. Come. We're waiting in Quinn's quarters."

"So Reid is here? At the palace?" Jarek asked, following Falke as he moved toward the door.

"He's been staying here for a month. Our queen demanded it until Jasmine had the babies."

"Babies?" Mei asked, catching the word.

"Yes," Falke nodded. "Twins."

"But," Mei blinked and touched her own stomach. Twins? She'd never thought of that. Suddenly, she was nervous.

"You are with child as well?" Falke asked, looking at where her hand hovered over her stomach. "This is truly a blessed day."

Jarek led her inside, stopping when he saw a man. "Tal, please tell my crew to wait in the dining hall. Have the servants get them drinks and tell them what is happening."

"Welcome back, Prince Jarek," Tal, a palace guard, answered before going out to greet the crew.

"It's beautiful," Mei said in awe, looking around the palace hall. If she thought the outside was impressive, the inside took her breath away. She was amazed to find herself staring at the intricate carvings over the arched doorways. There were particularly beautiful, symmetrical patterns of brilliantly displayed colors—blue, red, orange, gold, and green—inlaid into the walls.

"I will show it all to you later," Jarek promised. He grinned, clearly excited about the news of Reid's twins. For a couple of big, gruff warrior men, the brothers really did look extremely excited about the prospect of babies. Mei would never tell them, but she found it adorable.

The brothers led her quickly past two open doors leading to an empty banquet hall. From what she could see, it had a high domed glass ceiling and mosaic patterns on the walls and floor. Flowers swept over the walls in long garlands and over the long tables and bench seats. Mei tried to slow her step, but Jarek pulled her on.

"We're preparing the celebration for Reid and Jasmine tonight," Falke said, noting her attention. "And now we will celebrate your mating as well."

With each step, they seemed to walk faster until Mei was nearly jogging to keep up with their larger stride. Tripping, she gasped when Jarek swung her up into his arms, carrying her with him.

"I can walk," she protested.

"Ah, but I'd much rather carry you." He didn't set her down until they were at Prince Quinn's personal wing within the palace. Falke merely grinned as if such things were commonplace. Considering the almost barbaric air about the men, she assumed it most likely was. She was beginning to realize that Jarek's people were much more relaxed when it came to decorum.

Without knocking, Falke entered Quinn's home. "Look what I found!"

Mei remembered Jarek telling her that Prince Quinn was married to Princess Vittoria, or Tori as the family called her. Their home was simple in design, colored with rich blues and creams. The wide tiled floor stretched before the front door, elegant and immaculately clean. A couple of men sat on a low, wide couch near a raised platform before a large fireplace. Long pillows were laid out on the floor near their feet, perfect for lounging, which one man did. The man on the floor played with a baby. He was obviously the boy's father, as they looked exactly alike. Next to them, a black animal slept curled into a ball on the floor.

Aside from the front, there were no doors in the home. Tall decorative arches in the wall led to a bedroom, a kitchen, and another room. A wall of glass, so thick Mei couldn't see through it curved around one side of the room. An inlet next to the fireplace, near the kitchen, led to a large dining room.

At Falke's words, Jarek set her down on the floor. The men stood and hurried forward, excitedly greeting their space exploring brother with hugs and punches. One even grabbed Jarek by the neck and play wrestled with him.

A tiny little girl poked her head around the corner of the couch and squealed, "Da da!" She waddled to Falke, lifting up her pudgy arms and grinning with dimples in the most adorable chubby cheeks.

"A girl?" Jarek asked, in amazement, reaching to touch the child's hair. She smiled sweetly, sniffing at his hand before letting him touch her.

Falke grinned and presented his daughter. "Payton. Payton, this is your Uncle Jarek."

The little girl made a small noise of contentment and put her face in Jarek's large hand.

"She grows fast," Jarek observed, glancing from the girl to her baby cousin.

"Her mother is part Ticaron," Falke explained. "Already Payton speaks like a child twice her age."

"She really is one in a million," Mei said. Falke could not have been prouder as he nodded in agreement.

"Mei, this is King Kirill, and over there is his son, Korbin," Jarek said, motioning to a dark animal asleep on one of the pillows.

Kirill smiled at her. He had the same dark eyes as Jarek.

"And this is Quinn, our official Var ambassador," Jarek said, pointing to the man who'd come up from the floor. "And the little one with him is my nephew, Roderic."

Roderic held back, growling mischievously in the back of his throat. His eyes lit with the threat of a shift, and he grew little fangs. Turning in her father's arms, Payton opened her bowed little lips and let out a deafening roar. Mei jumped, startled by the ungodly sound coming from such a little thing.

"Payton," Falke scolded though parental pride was evident in him. "I told you, no roaring in the house."

"Torry, da da," she apologized, chewing on a finger.

"Did I hear Payton?" Another joined them. Mei stared as a man, eerily identical to her husband, came into the room. The only thing missing was Jarek's black markings on his arm and neck. "Jarek!"

"Reid," Jarek said, hurrying to hug his twin. "Congratulations, brother, on this wonderful day."

"Thank you," Reid said. "I can't believe you made it back. And today of all days."

Mei stood back, smiling. Seeing her, Falke cleared his throat, drawing the brothers' attention.

"Brothers, may I present to you Princess Mei, my wife," Jarek said.

"And she is with child," Falke added as if he couldn't keep the secret any longer.

Mei's heart fluttered in her chest. He looked so proud as he said the words. The already excited brothers broke out in rounds of congratulations and enthusiasm, demanding to know all about her. It really was a touching scene. Jarek answered for her the best he could amidst the commotion, which wasn't too much considering everyone was talking at once.

"Reid," a woman scolded, peeking out of the same room he'd come from moments before. Her red-blonde hair practically gleamed in the light coming from the fireplace. "I told you to keep everyone quiet. Jasmine's—"

A loud baby's cry interrupted her and the woman hurried back into the room without finishing. Reid ran after her, tripping over his feet to get back to his wife.

"Oh, Sacred cats," Reid hollered after a pause. "Jasmine?"

Jarek, Falke, Quinn and Kirill instantly were on guard, rushing the door.

"Ulyssa," Kirill ordered. As they tried to go in,

the same woman was there to meet them, instantly pushing the brothers out.

"Lyssa," Payton cooed happily.

"Quiet my little princess, all right?" the woman said. "Hush for Jas-jas."

"Jas-jas," Payton repeated softly, nodding.

"What is it, Ulyssa?" Quinn demanded. "Is Jasmine all right?"

"She's fine," said Ulyssa, who Mei knew was the queen.

"What's wrong?" Kirill asked, trying to get past his wife.

"Stay back," she ordered. "I can guarantee Jas will not be happy if you go barging in there now. And trust me, your own wives won't be too pleased with you either."

"Ah," a woman screamed. "Lys-s-a!"

"Get them out," another ordered. "Quinn, you'd better keep your brothers out of here."

"Yes, Tori," Quinn hollered. "I love you!"

"I love you, too," was the woman's answer. "Now quit talking. I have to concentrate."

"Sam?" Falke called.

"Yeah, yeah, I love you, too," Sam said.

"How is she?" Falke demanded.

"Everything's fine," Sam answered from the other side. "Leave us alone. Go away."

"Jarek's here," Falke yelled back. "And he's got a pregnant wife with him. She's as tiny as you are!"

"What?" the word was yelled in unison, in a chorus of female voices.

"I said, Jarek is here, and he brought a pregnant wife with him and she's as tiny as Sam—" Falke tried to repeat.

"We heard you the first time," Sam yelled. "Blessed stars, here it comes! You can do it, Jas. Tell her not to go anywhere. Jarek, you'd better not take your wife anywhere. We want to meet her."

Ulyssa pushed the men before going into the room once more. "Stay out." Then glancing at Mei, she waved and then disappeared through the doorway.

Mei wanted to laugh at how easily the women ordered about their husbands and the men seemed to listen to them quite well. They trailed back into the waiting area, still looking worried. Jarek came to her side, holding her close as all four big men stared at the door, waiting.

Suddenly Reid burst from the room. "Girls!"

"What?" the brothers said in unison.

"Twin girls," Reid proclaimed, holding a swaddled baby in the crook of each arm. "I swear it on our dead father. They're girls. I made Tori check them to make sure nothing fell off. It's definite. They're girls."

Mei tried not to choke on her laughter. Reid said it with such seriousness.

"They're lovely," Mei told him.

"Yeah," Reid agreed, completely enamored with his children, "they are, aren't they?"

"Um, I think now would be the best time to remind you of what you said to Falke the day Payton was born," Quinn said. "You're going to have your work cut out for you. There will be a lot of boys—"

He never finished the words. Reid paled, groaning loudly as he pulled his daughters closer. "You're right. We're going to have to tighten up security around here. And I'll have to find some female maids, perhaps from father's old harem brides. Oh, and they definitely aren't going to be leaving the palace." To his daughters, he cooed, "That's right, girls. Daddy's not going to let you out of his sight, ever."

"Reid, you will do no such thing." Ulyssa came out of the room followed by two women. She came forward, cooing to the babies, "Don't you worry sweethearts, Aunt Lyssa will make sure your mean old daddy doesn't keep you locked in a tower."

"A tower," Reid repeated. "Hey, you know, that's not a bad idea. Kirill, I'll need the palace architects to get started on a tower right away."

"But, you live in the outlands," Kirill said, arching a brow.

"Oh, right. Well, in that case, I'll need the architects to come out to the forest and build one there. And I'll need Falke to start training female guards."

Ulyssa rolled her eyes. "Reid, you are not hiring a bunch of female guards. In case you forgot, this is a male dominated planet. You're not going to find women that are equipped to fight."

"Eunuchs?" he suggested hopefully.

"Girls, you are so lucky you have us," Ulyssa said to the babies. Then, seeing Mei, she smiled. "You must be… Welcome to the family…ah?"

"This is my wife, Mei," Jarek said. "Mei, this is Ulyssa, Tori, and Sam."

Tori wore all black and had long dark hair and dark eyes. Sam was petite with short, choppy blond hair. A streak of purple slashed through the bangs. The lock fell forward over her face, partially hiding her round violet eyes. She wore pants and a tank shirt with cross laces like all of the men. A blue tattoo wound around her upper arm.

"And she's pregnant," Falke offered again.

Sam grinned up at her giant of a husband. "You're just a big softy, aren't you, baby?"

"Congratulations," Tori said. "We are so happy to meet you."

Princess Tori's sentiments were repeated by the others. The women instantly rushed forward in a scene very much like the one their husbands had put on when they'd found out.

"You have to tell us everything. How did you and Jarek meet? Where did you come from? Where can I get a skirt like that? It's gorgeous," Ulyssa exclaimed, taking Mei by the arm.

"You have to meet Jasmine," Tori said, taking her by the other arm. The women started leading her toward the door. "You can tell us all about how you and Jarek met and got together. And we'll tell you all about how we found our husbands. We'll be as close as sisters in no time."

Mei looked over her shoulder at Jarek, only to see the petite ex-Captain Sam confronting him.

"You've had her long enough, Jarek," Sam said, placing her hand on his chest. "It's our turn. We're going to make sure you didn't act like your brothers during the courtship. Trust me, if we find out you've been a royal ass, we'll be having a chat later."

"But," Jarek tried to protest. He looked powerlessly at Mei. She gave him a smile.

"Nope," Sam interrupted, holding up her hand and refusing to let him speak.

"I didn't—" he started.

"Ah, no, not a word," she said, stepping away.

The petite woman was little bigger than Mei, but she had a presence that could command a room. "We'll talk later." Then as an afterthought when she joined the others at the door, she said to him, "And you'd better have taken care of my crew. I miss that lot of misfits."

"They're in the hall, all safe and sound," Jarek assured her.

"They'd better be, or it's your head," Sam said.

"It's a good thing you got Rick back, isn't it *qin ài de?*" Mei winked mischievously at her husband, and he tried to shake his head to stop her.

"What? What happened to my Rick?" Sam demanded. Then motioning into the bedroom, she said, "Never mind. Come inside and meet Jasmine and you can tell us everything. We want all the details."

The men laughed.

"I'm glad it's you and not me," Reid said. "You are in for it now, brother."

"Yeah," Quinn agreed. "Trust me, when those women are mad...*whoa.* I don't even want to think about it."

"Give me a niece," Kirill demanded, crossing over to his brother. Before being dragged into the room to meet Princess Jasmine, Mei saw all five giant Var princes hovering over two very tiny little girls. Jarek looked at her, smiling brightly, his eyes so happy.

"I love you, *fea*," he mouthed.

Mei grinned, trying to answer, but her new friends swept her away too quickly. Her heart filled with the love from Jarek's family. It was in the very air around them.

The End

Find out what happens to Jarek's crew,
thanks to Rick's big mouth.

Space Lords Book 1: His Frost Maiden

The series continues

Empath and space pirate, Evan Cormier is obsessed with decoding an ominous premonition about his future. When a fellow crewman angered a spirit, the vengeful Zhang An took her wrath out on everyone in the vicinity. Evan just happened to be one of them. He's now facing a future in which he'll be forever alone.

Lady Josselyn of the House of Craven has been betrayed. With her home world on a Florencian moon under attack and her family dead, she finds herself at the mercy of the one who deceived them. There is only one thing left to do—die with honor. But before she can join her family in the afterlife, she must first avenge all that she held dear. Falling in love with a pirate was never in the plan. Evan and his thieving crewmates might have delayed her fate, but they can't stop destiny.

His Frost Maiden Excerpt

Craven Estates, Earth Settlement, Florencia's Fifth Moon

"Lift her," the General ordered, his shiny boots walking away from her, taking her reflection with it.

Two men hauled her to her feet, holding her up by her arms. Josselyn suppressed a cry as they jerked her dislocated shoulder. She couldn't see their faces, didn't need to. Her body hurt so badly she couldn't tell where the pain was coming from anymore.

The one who'd betrayed them stood before her. General Jack Stephans. He'd deceived her family and the fifth moon settlement. He'd traded them in for money and power. Josselyn lifted her gaze briefly to the hard depths of the steel green eyes before her. She wanted to kick, to give one last good blow, to go down fighting, but she couldn't raise her limbs.

"Poor little Josselyn, so heartbreaking," the General grabbed her chin and swiped beneath her eye. He looked young, was in fact very young for his position, only a few years older than her six and twenty. And yet they all knew so much more of fighting than anyone their age should, than anyone ever should.

"We gave you a home," she whispered. "How could you do this? How could you join them?"

"You gave me a place in your stables," he spat, his grip tightening on her chin, bruisingly so. "Not a place at your table. Not a place by your side. Not equal. They gave me a rank, a title. They give me respect. They give me a place in this world."

"Jack," she said, her voice softening for the orphan boy they'd found over twenty years ago. If she begged him, maybe fate could be turned around; maybe this day could be erased. Fate had spit them out in a whirlwind of chance and deceit. Maybe all that had happened wasn't his fault. Maybe it wasn't hers. None of it mattered. None of it changed the fact that he had taken everything she held dear, everyone, and now he was robbing her of her family home. Her tone hardened and she closed her eyes. "General."

"Look at me, Josselyn," he said. His tone

caught even as his grip on her face tightened until his fingers pressed the inside of her cheeks against her teeth. "You're so cold. Even now, your face is composed. Is one, lonely tear all the passion you can muster?"

"I am Lady Josselyn of the House of Craven." Her eyes opened slowly, focusing on the shiny white of his uniform. It gleamed with the orange glow coming from the fireplace. The material looked odd in the drabber earth tones many on the fifth moon wore. Theirs was a world based on Medieval Earth. Each moon in the Florencian system was different, each settlement patterned off a singular time in the human past, times that history had almost forgotten. But the principals of the ancestors who'd established the colonies no longer applied. Times were different now. What had started as preservation of history had turned into reality, into laws and a way of life they all believed in as generation after generation was raised into the worlds of the Florencian moons.

The General shook her by the face until finally she forced her eyes to meet his. He looked angry, hurt, wildly hopeful. "I can save you. I can say you had nothing to do with the treachery of your family. No one wants to kill a woman of noble blood. The line of Craven doesn't have to die. I will take your name; the name denied me by your father."

Was he serious? She knew he'd asked her father for her hand in marriage. In fact, she'd dismissed the proposal with the full knowledge he only asked because he wanted power. Did he think she could love him now? Want him? Take him into her bed?

He must have read the answer on her face because his own expression hardened. She knew Jack. He wouldn't ask again.

"I suppose not," he said, almost sad. "Even if you agreed, I could never trust you not to take a blade to my back. Not after today." He sighed heavily. "Not after this."

"Ago," she whispered, even her voice beginning to fail in its strength, "pugna quod int-"

"Quiet your tongue! This house is mine. Mine." He let go of her chin and her head drooped. "And you can die knowing that I have taken more than what you all refused to give me in life."

"A place at our table," Josselyn said, her tone softer still, the will to live leaving her. Her heart called out to her ancestors, to her dead family, begging them to come and get her.

"My table," he answered, stepping away. The General lifted a gun, pointing it at her head. She heard the telltale click of metal on metal. The weapon was not one found on the fifth moon. They fought with swords and axes, like the old medieval ways. Though technology was available, not using it was a point of honor. He must have brought the weapon from another moon. Perhaps the Victorians? The Elizabethans? It appeared to be too old to be from much later in time.

"Do it, Jack." She didn't look at him as she waited for the final discharge of the gun, the loud bang before the end. When it didn't come, she repeated, the words a mere mouthing of her lips, "Do it."

"Speed you to a quick end, Josselyn Craven," Jack whispered. "You all brought this on yourselves."

**To find out more about Michelle's books
visit www.MichellePillow.com**

Learn what happens to Mei's family...

Seduction of the Phoenix (Dynasty Lords 1)

The series continues

A prince raised in honor and tradition, a woman raised with nothing at all. She wants to steal their most sacred treasure. He'll do anything to protect it, even if it means marrying a thief.

Prince Zhang Jin is a man raised in honor and tradition, so it is a great surprise when he is compelled to claim a stranger as his bride who has neither. Francesca La Rosa is hardly a match fit for a prince. Though beautiful, she is a thief with one thing on her mind—stealing the sacred Jade Phoenix of his people. But the mystery doesn't end there. With the aid of the spirits of his ancestors he must discover who this woman is, why she would destroy the Zhang Empire and most of all, if she could ever return the love that is growing in his heart.

New York Times & *USA TODAY*
Bestselling Author

Michelle loves to travel and try new things, whether it's a paranormal investigation of an old Vaudeville Theatre or climbing Mayan temples in Belize. She believes life is an adventure fueled by copious amounts of coffee.

Newly relocated to the American South, Michelle is involved in various film and documentary projects with her talented director husband. She is mom to a fantastic artist. And she's managed by a dog and cat who make sure she's meeting her deadlines.

For the most part she can be found wearing pajama pants and working in her office. There may or may not be dancing. It's all part of the creative process.

Come say hello! Michelle loves talking with readers on social media!

www.MichellePillow.com

facebook.com/AuthorMichellePillow

twitter.com/michellepillow

instagram.com/michellempillow

bookbub.com/authors/michelle-m-pillow

goodreads.com/Michelle_Pillow

amazon.com/author/michellepillow

youtube.com/michellepillow

pinterest.com/michellepillow

COMPLIMENTARY EXCERPTS

them. When the men aren't bragging about how they're going to marry her, they're acting like she's a delicate rare flower in need of their protection.

She is far from a shrinking solarflower.

Prince Llyr of the Draig knows four things for a fact: He is the future king of the dragon-shifters. He must act honorably in all ways. He absolutely, positively is meant to marry Lady Mede. And she dead set against marriage.

Llyr's fate rests in the hands of a woman determined not to have any man. With a new threat emerging amongst their cat-shifting neighbors, a threat whose eyes are focused firmly on Mede, time may be running out. It is up to him to convince her to be his dragon queen.

For a complete, up-to-date booklist, visit www.MichellePillow.com

Warlocks MacGregor Book 1

Contemporary Paranormal Scottish Warlocks

A little magickal mischief never hurt anyone…

Erik MacGregor, from a clan of ancient Scottish warlocks, isn't looking for love. After centuries, it's not even a consideration…until he moves in next door to Lydia Barratt. It's clear that the shy beauty wants nothing to do with him, but he's drawn to her nonetheless and determined to win her over.

Lydia Barratt just wants to be left alone to grow flowers and make lotions in her old Victorian house. The last thing she needs is a demanding Scottish man meddling in her private life. Just because he's gorgeous and totally rocks a kilt doesn't mean she's going to fall for his seductive manner.

But Erik won't give up and just as Lydia let's her guard down, his sister decides to get involved. Her little love potion prank goes terribly wrong, making Lydia the target of his sudden embarrassingly obsessive behavior. They'll have to find a way to pull Erik out of the spell fast when it becomes clear that Lydia has more than a lovesick warlock to worry about. Evil lurks within the shadows and it plans to use Lydia, alive or dead, to take out Erik and his clan for good.

Love Potions Excerpt

"Ly-di-ah! I sit beneath your window, laaaass, singing 'cause I loooove your a——"

"For the love of St. Francis of Assisi, someone call a vet. There is an injured animal screaming in pain outside," Charlotte interrupted the flow of music in ill-humor.

Lydia lifted her forehead from the kitchen table. Her windows and doors were all locked, and yet Erik's endlessly verbose singing penetrated the barrier of glass and wood with ease.

Charlotte held her head and blinked heavily.

Her red-rimmed eyes were filled with the all too poignant look of a hangover. She took a seat at the table and laid her head down. Her moan sounded something like, "I'm never moving again."

"You need fluids," Lydia prescribed, getting up to pour unsweetened herbal tea from the pitcher in the fridge. She'd mixed it especially for her friend. It was Gramma Annabelle's hangover recipe of willow bark, peppermint, carrot, and ginger. The old lady always had a fresh supply of it in the house while she was alive. Apparently, being a natural witch also meant in partaking in natural liquors. Annabelle had kept a steady supply of moonshine stashed in the basement. If the concert didn't stop soon she might try to find an old bottle.

"*Ly-di-ah!*"

"Omigod. Kill me," Charlotte moaned. "No. Kill him. Then kill me."

"*Ly-di-ah!*"

Erik had been singing for over an hour. At first, he'd tried to come inside. She'd not invited him and the barrier spell sent him sprawling back into the yard. He didn't seem to mind as he found a seat on some landscaping timbers and began his serenade. The last time she'd asked him to be quiet, he'd gotten louder and overly enthusiastic. In fact, she'd been too scared to pull back the curtains for a clearer look, but she was pretty sure he'd been dancing on her lawn, shaking his kilt.

"Omigod," Charlotte muttered, pushing up and angrily going to a window. Then grimacing, she said, "Is he wearing a tux jacket with his kilt?"

"Don't let him see you," Lydia cried out in a panic. It was too late. The song began with renewed force.

"He's…" Charlotte frowned. "I think it's dancing."

Since the damage was done, Lydia joined Charlotte at the window. Erik grinned. He lifted his arms to the side and kicked his legs, bouncing around the yard like a kid on too much sugar. "Maybe it's a traditional Scottish dance?"

Both women tilted their heads in unison as his kilt kicked up to show his perfectly formed ass.

"He's not wearing…" Charlotte began.

"I know. He doesn't," Lydia answered. Damn, the man had a fine body. Too bad Malina's trick had turned him insane.

**To find out more about Michelle's books
visit www.MichellePillow.com**